For anyone else who ever wished
for a pony but is still waiting
P. F.

Text copyright © 2018 by Polly Faber
Illustrations copyright © 2018 by Sarah Jennings

First US edition 2020
First published by Walker Books (UK) 2018

Library of Congress Catalog Card Number pending
ISBN 978-1-5362-0930-3

20 21 22 23 24 25 LBM 10 9 8 7 6 5 4 3 2 1

Printed in Melrose Park, IL, U.S.A.

Candlewick Press
99 Dover Street
Somerville, Massachusetts 02144

www.candlewick.com

MIX
From responsible
sources
FSC® C103098

A JUNIOR LIBRARY GUILD SELECTION

PONY ON THE TWELFTH FLOOR

POLLY FABER

illustrated by SARAH JENNINGS

CANDLEWICK PRESS

CHAPTER ONE

Kizzy thought she had dreamed of every possible way she might get a pony. She'd never expected to pick one up from the grocery store.

Kizzy had only stopped to get milk and pasta. She was with her best friend, Pawel, and he was rolling his eyes as she demonstrated how to clear obstacles on a show-jumping course. Kizzy, her skirt hitched up, had successfully jumped a low wall of cereal boxes on a two-for-one deal and was cantering down the aisle toward a display of toilet paper. And there it was. A pony.

She swerved abruptly and stopped. Toilet paper scattered everywhere.

"Is that a refusal or a knockdown? Not a clear round anyway. You get four points either way . . ." Pawel was saying, when he saw it, too. "Oh!"

"Faults, Pawel," whispered Kizzy. "How many times: it's faults, not points! But . . . please tell me this is real and not a mirage in my horse desert!"

She edged toward the pony, her hand stretched out in wonder. It was bathed in a shaft of sunlight. The tinny background music playing in the grocery store sounded like a choir of angels.

The pony looked surprisingly at home in the bakery section. Its nose was buried in a tray of donuts, which it was devouring quickly. It was plump and chestnut colored, with a pale golden tail and a shaggy mane that fell over dark, heavily lashed eyes. Kizzy had never seen anything more beautiful.

A lead rope trailed on the ground from the pony's halter. Kizzy closed her gaping mouth and looked around for the person who should have been holding the other end. There was nobody in sight.

"Hey! Who let that animal in here? It's service dogs only."

A wary-looking security guard popped up at the other end of the aisle. He waved his arms around uncertainly. "Whoa! Shoo! Away with you!" Shoplifting ponies had probably not been included in his training, Kizzy thought. The pony lifted its head from the donuts, shook out its mane, causing a small shower of multi-colored sprinkles to fall from its whiskers, and took a single step toward the guard.

The guard shrieked, stumbled backward, and tipped bottom first into the open chest freezer behind him. "Aargh! It's savage! It's coming for me!" Floundering in the freezer, he grabbed a box of frozen waffles and brandished it in front of him like a shield. The pony paused and considered the waffles, then turned back to the tray of donuts and resumed eating.

Kizzy made a decision. She picked up the pony's trailing rope. "It's OK," she reassured the guard. "You're quite safe. I've got him again now. He belongs to me." She wasn't even sure the pony *was* a he. It didn't seem the right moment to check.

Pawel stared at Kizzy. He didn't speak, but his look said plenty.

"I'm really sorry," continued Kizzy, ignoring Pawel. "He got away from me. I think it was the smell—you know, the baking smell wafting out through the doors. It always makes me hungry, and I'm afraid my pony couldn't help himself and decided to come in . . . and help himself. We'll be on our way now, and we'll pay

for these." Kizzy spread out her hand and indicated the donuts and a tray of apple pastries beneath that had also been attacked by pony teeth.

Pawel offered his arm to the security guard to help him out of the freezer. He began to brush ice crystals and stray frozen peas off the man's uniform, but the guard angrily batted him away. Judging by the guard's face, Kizzy thought it would be sensible for them to leave the grocery store as soon as possible.

She led the pony away. With one last snatch at the pastries, the pony followed happily. Pawel was still ominously silent, but Kizzy kept talking enough for both of them.

"I only just got him, so I'm still learning. I'm very sorry. It won't happen again. Excuse us. Move out of the way, please. Thank you!" They waited awkwardly behind a line of staring shoppers, then Kizzy put a handful of change down in front of the cashier. "That should cover it. We don't need a bag, thank you. Lovely day, isn't it? See you soon!"

"Unexpected pony in the bagging area," muttered the cashier as they departed.

Once the automatic doors had closed behind them, Pawel found his voice. "Kizzy! What are you DOING? 'My pony'? Did you just STEAL a pony? It's a pony! A PONY. You CAN'T have a pony!"

Kizzy straightened up from where she'd been checking under the pony's considerable stomach. "Yes, he is a he." She smoothed her hand along the pony's broad flank. "I know very well he's a pony, Pawel. And I haven't stolen him. I've . . . taken charge of him temporarily. Someone had to. Until his real owner is found. Although they can't be a very good owner if they managed to lose him in a supermarket, can they?"

"Right." Pawel looked dubious.

The three of them stood together on the sidewalk. Cars, trucks, buses—all the usual rush hour city traffic was crawling past. In the middle of the concrete and street signs and pavement and gas fumes, the pony looked as out of place as he had in the supermarket. But he was unfazed by the noise and vehicles. He stood peacefully, chewing his last morsels of pilfered snacks.

"What's a pony doing in Hope Green anyway?"

Pawel asked. "And what are we supposed to do with him now? Should we walk him down to the police station and see if they'll take care of him? I can't be late; I've got to help with the twins and there's lots of homework."

Kizzy wasn't listening. She was lost in her new friend's big brown eyes. She put her arms around the pony's soft, strong neck, pressed the side of her face against it, and breathed deeply. He smelled of dreams come true. She wondered when entries closed for the show jumping at the National Horse Show and started mentally rearranging her bedroom shelves to make space for the trophies they would win.

"Hmm? Yes, we could do that. I could do that. If you're busy, why don't you go home and I'll let you know what they say?"

"You will take him to the police, won't you, Kizzy?" Pawel gave her a penetrating look as he tentatively patted the pony goodbye. "I'll call you at six, OK? Maybe there'll even be a reward and you'll get your picture on the news or something!"

"Yes, maybe I will . . ." said Kizzy, still dreaming of cups and rosettes. "Don't worry; I'll take care of him."

She'd wished and waited for this moment forever. Living in an apartment in the city, Kizzy had always known the odds of her getting a pony were slimmer than those of the children in her favorite pony books. So far, Kizzy had spent eleven years of her life without putting out a single fire in a hay barn to earn the lifelong gratitude of a pony-owning farmer, or finding the opportunity to buy a neglected mare at auction for a bargain, or rescuing an abandoned mustang foal from the jaws of a coyote. But now it had happened. For one evening at least, Kizzy decided, this magical gift pony could be hers.

"Where did you come from?" she asked the pony once Pawel had gone. "Do I have a secret fairy godmother who magicked you up? You're not from anywhere near here. There are no ponies near here." The pony cocked his ears back and forth as if he was listening but revealed no secrets. "What shall I call you?" continued Kizzy. She tried out horse names from her books. "Daydream? Sweetbriar? Storm Warning?"

None of them seemed quite right for the solid, shaggy-coated shape by her side. This gift pony didn't seem to have Arab or thoroughbred blood or the high-spirited nature that Kizzy had been led to believe was usual in gift ponies. She thought back to their first meeting. "Shall we call you Donut?"

The pony didn't object. It was settled. Kizzy and Donut set off for home.

CHAPTER TWO

Kizzy and Donut wandered along the street, stopping every so often as the pony lowered his head to steal mouthfuls of grass from the side of the road and occasional chunks of bushes, too. Kizzy's arms were nearly pulled out of their sockets when he lunged for the marigolds in the hanging baskets outside the Fox and Chickens pub.

"Now, Donut, that's not allowed. All my books on horse management say it's wrong to let you eat whatever you want. What if those plants were poisonous?" Kizzy tried to sound commanding. The pony kept on snatching and chewing. He seemed to know what he was doing.

She was taking him the long way home, carefully avoiding Sunshine Café—her mom worked there. As she passed the pet shop, Kizzy felt in her pocket for her wallet. She wanted to be a responsible owner. Holding on to Donut's lead while he trimmed the grass tufts around a tree outside, Kizzy stuck her head in the door.

"How much is hay, please?" she asked the man at the counter.

"For a rabbit, is it? Five dollars a bale," he said, not looking up from his phone.

Kizzy counted what she had left. It would mean spending all the money Mom had given her for food shopping. She'd worry about that later. Her pony (*her* pony!) was more important.

"Can you bring it over?" she asked, straining forward to put her money on the counter.

"What's on the end of the rope?" asked the man. "Must be a big rabbit."

He grabbed a bale of hay and passed it over. Kizzy looked at it. It didn't seem like very much. She hadn't known Donut long, but she had a feeling he'd get through it quickly. And how would she buy more? Another thing to worry about later.

She walked off with Donut. The man's attention was already back on his phone. By the time he'd glanced up — confused by the size of the shadow passing the door — they had gone.

Approaching her building, Kizzy saw another problem: a crowd of Jem's friends were outside playing football. At least there was no sign of her brother with them.

"We'll have to hide, Donut. They'll probably go away in a bit and then we'll make a run for it."

Donut and Kizzy waited around the corner, in the shadow cast by Kizzy's building. The pony put his head down and helped himself to more clumps from the grassy yard. Kizzy sat and watched him. Her heart was full. That she, Kezia Arnott, should have her very own pony (for a little while at least, all right?) at last. She wondered again where he'd come from. A picture of a weeping owner searching the streets came to her. Kizzy pushed that thought away. She was going to be the best owner Donut could ever want. She'd train him and groom him and love him, and together they would ride on magnificent adventures and gallop across fields and win competitions and—

Donut interrupted her thoughts by releasing a stream of fizzing urine. It trickled down the slope toward where she was sitting. Kizzy jumped to her feet just in time. She hadn't really thought about the pee. He produced a very large amount for a small horse. She wondered when he would need to do another one and how best to prepare for it. Perhaps she could walk him around the block the last thing at night and first thing in the morning, like people did with dogs.

"WHAT ARE YOU UP TO? RUINING MY LAWN? CLEAR OFF!"

Kizzy spun around. It was Mr. Newman, the building super—but it was Jem's friends he was yelling at. They picked up their ball and shuffled off grumbling while Mr. Newman watched from the front door, his sleeves rolled up and his hands on his hips. And then they were gone, and Mr. Newman disappeared back inside.

Kizzy counted slowly to fifty to give him a chance to settle back in his apartment. She knew he liked to watch game shows at this time. It was now or never. She pulled at Donut's head.

"Come on. Time to go home. Quick now." Tugging him away from the grass, Kizzy moved toward the main entrance. She propped open the swing doors and made a clicking noise to coax the pony through.

Donut's hooves clattered across the concrete lobby floor. Kizzy could hear the laughter of a game show audience through the door of Mr. Newman's apartment. There was a strong smell of deep frying wafting from inside. Donut stopped for a moment and turned toward the temptation.

"NO, Donut!" Kizzy hissed. "This way." She pressed the button for the elevator, praying that it would be empty. There was a ping, the metal doors opened, and Kizzy breathed a sigh of relief. She led Donut inside and pressed the button for the twelfth floor.

After maneuvering Donut safely out of the elevator and into the apartment, Kizzy made some adjustments to turn her bedroom into an emergency stable. First, she squeezed Donut into the bathroom and filled the bath up in case he wanted a drink. He only just fit through

the doorway. He wasn't too tall, but he was almost too
wide. She rushed around, putting away her precious
china horses, rolling up her rug, and clearing the floor.
Remembering the pee, she found a tarp in a closet from
when they painted the family room and laid it on the
floor with all of the guest towels. She hoped they would
catch some of what Donut produced; she couldn't risk
a damp patch appearing on the ceiling of the apartment

below. Lastly, Kizzy made a hay net from her gym bag and strung it up from the hook she used for her bath-robe. Transferred into his new accommodations, Donut showed his approval and immediately began to work through the hay.

The front door slammed. Kizzy froze. "Super quiet now, Donut." She held her finger to her lips.

"Kizz! You in?" Jem, her brother, shouted from

the hallway. The handle on her bedroom door pressed down.

"Don't come in! I'm changing!" Kizzy yelled, practically throwing herself off her bed and squeezing around Donut to lunge for the door. The pony backed up and knocked into the desk, sending her lamp tumbling to the floor with a crash.

The handle flicked back up. "All right, calm down! Just saying hello. Want a drink? I've got some Coke. Do we need to start anything for dinner?"

Kizzy slipped out of her bedroom, shutting the door tightly behind her. Jem grinned and ruffled her messy hair. "Hello, squirtle. Thought you said you were changing out of your uniform?"

"I changed my mind," said Kizzy. "Yes please to Coke." She followed him into the kitchen, trying to look completely normal and not like somebody who was hiding a pony in her bedroom.

There was a loud thump from behind her as Donut flicked a hoof against the wall. Kizzy looked at her lanky brother nervously. Luckily he had put his headphones back on. He nodded his head in time to whatever he was listening to and gave her a thumbs-up as he poured them both a glass of Coke.

Kizzy suddenly remembered the milk and pasta she was supposed to have bought instead of hay and already-eaten donuts. She looked in the fridge. It wasn't inspiring. Her mom went food shopping on Saturdays, so they were always down to the last morsels on Fridays. All that was left today was the lump of cheese that had been meant for the pasta, a couple of carrots, and some strawberry yogurt tubes. Kizzy slipped the carrots into her pocket for Donut. Dinner was looking tricky. Not that Kizzy was hungry. She would happily live off old cheese and strawberry yogurt forever if it meant keeping her pony.

There was the sound of a key in the door. "Home!" called her mom. Kizzy glanced toward her bedroom door as her mom came down the hallway, but Donut stayed quiet. "Hello, you two. How were your days? And what's that smell? Jem, how many times do I need to tell you: put your sneakers out on the balcony when you take them off!"

Kizzy looked down at her brother's feet and saw

they were still safely contained in their sneakers. She sniffed. She knew where the smell was coming from.

"Just getting something from my room, Mom," she said, sidling away.

"Did you start the pasta already? Because I've brought some sandwiches home from work, so maybe those would be nicer for tonight." Her mom was looking in the fridge. "That's funny; I'm sure we had some carrots left. Has one of you spontaneously been eating vegetables? It's a miracle. Never mind, I'll open a can of corn."

In her room, Kizzy saw Donut had produced a pile of steaming poop balls, right in the middle of the tarp. She climbed onto her chair and opened the window as far as was allowed on the twelfth floor, which wasn't much, then got her school backpack and carefully emptied everything out of its biggest compartment. Using a pair of dirty socks as makeshift gloves, she picked up the warm poop, ball by ball, transferred it into the backpack, and zipped it up tight. She hoped that would get rid of most of the smell.

As Kizzy cleaned up, Donut nosed up to her. Kizzy felt he was really starting to trust her now. Even if she did find his real owner, perhaps he would refuse to go back to them? He might choose to stay by her side forever. She got her hairbrush and began to brush Donut's coat to make him silky smooth and shiny. After dinner she thought she might try braiding his mane. It looked like it would take even more detangling than her own hair.

"We both need conditioner, Donut. It's another sign we're meant for each other," Kizzy said. "I love you," she added quietly.

The pony turned his head and nuzzled her. Everything was perfect.

Then Donut made a sudden lunge.

His soft nuzzle turned into hard teeth fastening around Kizzy's skirt pocket. With a deft tug Donut tore the material and carrots from her side and crunched down on both together.

"Yikes! Donut! What are you doing?" Kizzy leaped away and looked down at the ragged hole he'd ripped in her uniform. He'd only just missed taking a chunk of her thigh off as well.

Donut answered with a rumbling whicker of contentment deep in his throat.

"Dinner's ready, Kizzy!" her mom called. "Where are you?"

"One minute," Kizzy called back. She took off her ruined skirt, shoved it into the back of her closet, and hastily pulled on her jeans. As she went to the door, Kizzy looked back at Donut. He was making happy teeth-grinding-carrot noises.

He didn't look sorry at all.

CHAPTER THREE

Kizzy realized being a secret pony owner was not going to make for a relaxing evening. Sliding into her chair at the dinner table, she found Jem already munching on his sandwich.

"*Now* you get changed," he said.

"She's becoming a teenager already," said their mom. "Having one in the house is bad enough. Don't forget to, you know, chew your food, Jem. Has that disappeared already?"

"Hungry," said Jem, licking the remaining crumbs directly off his plate. "Are there more?"

Jem had a lot in common with Donut, Kizzy thought.

Her phone vibrated, flashing Pawel's name. She wanted to ignore it, but—

"Go ahead, answer him. Don't worry about us," said her mom. "If you're going to go all teenage, you might as well do it right. Say hi to him for me." She grinned at Kizzy.

"No fair!" said Jem. "You never let me use my phone at the table!"

"Aw, having a phone is new for Kizz and it's Friday. I'm feeling generous."

Kizzy reluctantly picked up her phone.

"Hi, Pawel," she said. Her mom and Jem watched her, smiling and scowling, respectively.

"So . . ." he said.

"What?"

"What HAPPENED? With the police, Kizz. Did they take the pony? Who does he belong to? Did you have to make a report and stuff? Will you be on the news?"

"Not exactly," said Kizzy.

"What does 'not exactly' mean? Not exactly for being on the news or not exactly for making the report? Kizzy—"

"It's complicated."

"How complicated?"

"Quite complicated," admitted Kizzy. "Look, it's not a great time right now. We're having dinner. How about I meet you tomorrow morning in the park? I'll explain everything then."

"Ooo-oo-oooh. It's 'complicated' and Kizzy's meeting her boyfriend in the park," said Jem over the remains of his second sandwich. Kizzy stuck her tongue out at him.

"Sorry, Pawel. I've really got to go. I'll text you, OK?"

"You're being very mysteri—" began Pawel, but Kizzy pressed the button to cut him off.

"That was brief," said her mom, looking concerned. "Did you two have an argument?"

"No," said Kizzy. There was a crash from her bedroom. This time they all heard it.

"Oh! What was that?" asked her mom.

Kizzy jumped to her feet. "Just something falling off my desk, probably—it's a mess in there, but I'll clean it up. You can have the rest of my sandwich if you want, Jem. OK if I go and do my homework, Mom?"

"Don't you want to watch *Make Me a Superstar*?" asked her mom. "I don't know—bedroom cleaning and homework on a Friday night and disappearing carrots. It must be your hormones kicking in, because you're acting very strange."

Kizzy dropped a kiss on her mom's head and rushed back to her room.

Donut had turned around in the small space. In doing so, he'd knocked an old box of Legos off her desk: multicolored bricks were scattered all over the floor. He'd also managed to tear through Kizzy's favorite poster of a gray stallion galloping along a moonlit beach. The stallion was now missing his tail and one of his legs.

"Donut! NO!" hissed Kizzy, followed by a loud "OW!" as she stepped on a Lego.

Hopping on one foot, Kizzy was horrified to hear her mom's chair scraping as she got up from the table. She limped over to the bedroom door and prepared to throw herself on her knees and beg if her mom should come investigating.

Then she heard the noise of the TV turning on. Kizzy let out the breath she'd been holding. Hopefully nobody would overhear anything else now. She petted Donut's neck, hugged him, and twirled her fingers through his mane. Her pony was a miracle. Maybe he couldn't stay in her bedroom forever, but for now, despite the ruined school skirt and torn poster, there was nowhere in the world better for him to be. Kizzy picked up her hairbrush, selected a few ribbons from her drawer, and started on Donut's braids. Tonight was going to be the best sleepover ever.

At seven o'clock the next morning, Kizzy crept out of her bedroom and checked that the coast was clear. Jem wasn't going to be a problem: she could hear his snores rumbling through his bedroom door from here. He wouldn't surface for another five hours. Her mom was another matter.

Kizzy hovered outside her doorway for a moment or two, listening. Her mom seemed to be asleep but you could never be sure. They would have to tiptoe and

Kizzy wasn't sure tiptoeing was something ponies did. She went back to her room.

Ten minutes later, she came out again, this time leading Donut. She'd stretched as many of her navy blue school socks as she could find over his hooves to try to muffle the noise. They didn't exactly fit: Donut wore a larger size than Kizzy in socks.

Very, very slowly Kizzy opened the front door.

"Kizzy? That you? What time is it?" a sleepy voice called out from the darkness of her mom's bedroom.

Kizzy froze.

"Early, Mom. Everything's fine. Go back to sleep. I'm just going out for a run." Kizzy tugged frantically at Donut's halter. Thankfully, he followed her out the door.

"Mmmm-hmmm," said her mom, drifting back under.

Kizzy shut the front door, retrieved her socks, and pushed the elevator button. She watched the light blinking up to her from the ground floor, checking that it wasn't stopping on the way. This early on a Saturday was likely to be quiet, but she still chewed the end of her hair nervously as they waited. Donut nibbled at an itch under one of his socks.

The doors opened and the elevator was empty. But someone had dropped half a bag of chips in the corner. As Kizzy led him in, Donut's head shot forward to investigate, sending his bottom cannoning into the buttons on the other side and pressing every single one. As a result, the elevator stopped at every floor on the way down. Kizzy squirmed as the doors opened again and again. She tried to spread herself out as wide as she could at the front. If anyone was waiting, perhaps they might not notice Donut? Luckily they reached the bottom without her pony-hiding skills being put to the test.

It was on the last stretch across the lobby that disaster struck. Donut lifted his tail and — *plop, plop, plop* — produced a fresh trail of droppings. The balls scattered through the hall and past Mr. Newman's apartment. Kizzy watched them roll away; one came to a rest right on the super's doormat.

Her first thought was to clean up quickly, but Donut

had other ideas. The scent of fresh grass was in his nostrils, and nothing was going to stop him from getting to it. He snorted and pulled. Kizzy dug her heels in but found herself sliding along the floor and out through the doors. Donut was strong.

Kizzy knew she couldn't leave the lobby in that state. Mr. Newman would get up and start his morning building maintenance checks at any moment. And, although the front lobby was often a bit of a mess after the comings and goings of a Friday night, there was no way he wasn't going to wonder about horse poop.

Donut was already head down and grazing. Kizzy tied his rope to the metal sign that said CONSTABLE TOWERS. NO BALL GAMES and nipped back inside. She unzipped her backpack, already ripe from the previous night's load, and began adding in the morning's fresh offerings. She was picking the last ball up, the one on the doormat, when Mr. Newman opened his front door. It was a horrible shock for them both, not the least because he was in his pajamas.

"What do you think you're up to?" Mr. Newman

narrowed his eyes and scowled at Kizzy, who was still crouched down. She hid Donut's poop behind her back. "You spying on me? Planning early morning mischief?"

"No, Mr. Newman. Not at all. I was just picking up trash. You know . . . cleaning." Kizzy smiled extra brightly.

"Cleaning? Picking up trash? At this time of the morning? What kind of idiot do you take me for?"

"It's for school. Honest. For a . . . um . . . Hope Green Primary Ambassador in the Community Award. I thought I'd get started early." Kizzy tried to meet his gaze and not think about the still warm poop in her fist or the pony tethered just out of Mr. Newman's sight.

"Humph!" Mr. Newman looked a little less fierce. "If you want to be a Hope Green thingummy in the whatsit, you can mop the floors for me later. Come back after breakfast. Smells even worse than usual this morning. Someone must have dropped a kebab last night— that always lingers. Anyway, I need to start breakfast . . . and get dressed."

He disappeared back inside.

Kizzy let out a deep sigh of relief and relaxed her clenched hand. Ew! It wasn't pretty. She picked up her now groaning backpack and went outside.

Donut was just where she'd left him. That was good. What was less good was that he had company. An old lady was patting his neck and whispering in his ear. Kizzy recognized her as Miss Turney, who lived on the floor above them. Kizzy sometimes heard her walking around in the middle of the night. She kept strange hours generally; Jem said she was odd. Mom said she was on her own and it was sad and one day they should invite her over, but they never had. Kizzy had always found her a little frightening and tried to keep out of her way.

But Donut seemed to like her. He was eating a cookie she'd given him and nuzzling the pockets of her maroon quilted coat. Kizzy hoped the pockets were securely stitched.

"Is this your pony, dear?" asked Miss Turney. "He's a beauty, isn't he?"

"Yes," said Kizzy. "I mean, no. I mean, yes, he is a

beauty; but no, he's not mine. I'm taking care of him for a while. My mom said I could," she added. It wasn't likely her mom would talk to Miss Turney, but it was better to be safe.

"Ah, you don't see horses now, not like you used to. Once there were several around here. My dad had one for his fruit and vegetable stand. Took him to the market each morning—his name was Robbie. We kept him in the back and I used to help take care of him. He had a temper." Miss Turney ran her hands down Donut's back, smiling. She gave him another cookie.

Kizzy untied Donut's lead rope. "I wish there still were lots of ponies around. It must have been great. Thanks for watching him, Miss Turney. Sorry he ate all your cookies."

Miss Turney looked down vaguely at the empty bag in her hands. "Oh, that's all right, dear. I don't know why I brought them out with me. Must have known I'd meet a pony who wanted a treat!" The old lady giggled and suddenly looked much younger. Kizzy giggled with her. "Anyway, I'd better be on my way. Bye-bye, horsey!

That girl will take good care of you. So nice to have a pony," she added to Kizzy.

"Oh, it is," said Kizzy, throwing her arms around Donut and covering him in kisses. He smelled sweeter than ever. "It is," she whispered.

CHAPTER FOUR

At the park, Kizzy found Pawel pushing his sisters, six-year-old twins Ali and Lopa, on the swings. Pawel had taken them out early to escape the cries of their new brother, Marek, who had chronic colic. It hadn't been a restful few months for Pawel's family.

Pawel looked up, saw Donut, and stopped pushing. The two girls jumped off the swings and ran toward the pony, their arms circling in excitement.

"Kizzy! KIZZY! Whatcha got? A HORSE! Look, Pawel—KIZZY'S GOT A REAL HORSE!" they cried.

Donut backed up a little at their approach. It wasn't surprising—they were both wearing animal onesies, Ali a lion and Lopa a cheetah. Donut looked like a zebra surrounded by predators on the African savanna.

"Easy, Donut. They're wild, but they're friendly." Kizzy patted the pony's neck reassuringly. "Slow down a little, you two."

"Can we hug him? Can we ride him? Can we take him for a walk? Can we feed him?" The girls petted Donut.

"Yes. Most of those things, anyway." Kizzy was looking at Pawel, who was making his way over. He was full of different questions.

"I knew it," he said. "I just knew it. 'Complicated,' you said. You never went to the police at all, did you? What did you do with him overnight? Where did you find a stable?"

"The police wouldn't have been the right place for him. I looked it up on my phone. You have to report found animals to the city," said Kizzy.

Pawel narrowed his eyes. "Where did you keep the pony last night?"

Kizzy swallowed. "In my bedroom. It was fine.

There was plenty of space and he was perfectly happy. His name's Donut, by the way. At least, that's what I'm calling him and he likes it. Don't you, Donut?"

Donut was sniffing Lopa's hair in an interested way. Kizzy saw there was a bit of Lopa's breakfast stuck in it. She tugged Donut's head away before he could munch down on either oatmeal or hair. She was getting good at horse management.

"You kept him in your *bedroom*? Your bedroom on the twelfth floor of Constable Towers? Not some other massive bedroom I don't know about?"

Kizzy kept her chin up. "Yep."

"OK." There was a silence. "And your mom and Jem were fine with that?"

There was a longer silence. Kizzy's chin dropped.

"You didn't tell them?!" Pawel shook his head slowly. "You've stolen a horse, Kizz. You're a criminal and going to jail, and I'll only be able to visit you once a month and I won't have anyone to sit next to in math. Don't think I'm going to dig a tunnel to spring you out, either."

"I'm not going to jail because I haven't stolen a pony," said Kizzy. "I will report Donut later today — if you'll watch him while I do it. They're only open a couple of hours on Saturdays and it's still too early. I . . . oh honestly, Pawel — how often will I get to take care of a pony? I wanted one day. That's all."

"Stop being mean, Pawel," said Ali. "And, Kizzy, if you can't report him till later, does that mean you can ride him first?"

"Yes, yes, yes!" Lopa jumped up and down. "Ride Donut, Kizzy! We want to watch you ride!"

The park was becoming busier with joggers and dog walkers, and Donut was getting some curious looks. To be more private, the four of them left the park via an underpass at the back and brought Donut to an empty lot behind some empty industrial units. It had once been where Hope Green's huge metal gas tank sat; now the land was going to be auctioned to build apartments.

It was overgrown with grass and weeds and hidden away. The imprint made by the iron circle that had

surrounded the gas storage tank was still visible. It made a perfect riding arena.

Of course Kizzy wanted to ride Donut. That was the whole point. That was how they would gallop over open country with the wind in their hair and mane. That was how they would jump impossible fences and be picked for the Olympic team. That was how she and Donut would communicate without words, earning applause and gasps of wonder as they moved together like two halves of a whole. Of course she wanted to ride him. But . . .

"I'm not sure whether I should. What if he's not been broken yet?" she said.

"He's wearing shoes—doesn't that mean he's probably been ridden? Plus he doesn't seem very excitable or scared by traffic or anything." Pawel was logical.

"We don't have a saddle or bridle for him," said Kizzy.

"We saw ponies at the circus and they weren't wearing saddles when the lady in the feathers and sparkles stood on them, and you're only going to sit." Ali was encouraging.

"I don't have a helmet."

"You can use Pawel's bike helmet. That'll keep you safe." Lopa was helpful.

"Go on, Kizzy. This is your moment. What are you waiting for?" asked Pawel.

"The thing is . . ." began Kizzy. "The thing is . . ." She took a deep breath. "The thing is—I've never actually ridden a pony before."

Nobody spoke.

"I mean, there was a donkey once at the beach when I was five. And I've read lots about it and I think about riding all the time and I know all the theory but . . ." Kizzy tried to swallow the lump in her throat.

Donut exhaled in a bored way, shifted his weight from one foot to the other, lifted his tail, and farted. It was unexpectedly reassuring.

Pawel patted Kizzy on the back. "It's all right. I knew it really. But you've got to start somewhere if you're going to be a professional rider one day. We'll hold his head, and it's not very far to the ground if you fall off."

Kizzy made herself nod. "OK. I'll see if he'll let me get on him to start with."

The first problem was how to mount. He wasn't a particularly big pony—maybe twelve and a half hands, Kizzy estimated—but then Kizzy wasn't big, either. Plus Donut's sides were curved (his body was more or less spherical), and they were surprisingly slippery, too. Pawel tried to give her a leg up, but Kizzy couldn't get a grip. They both lost their balance and fell backward in a heap on the ground.

Donut stood still, waiting patiently while they picked themselves up. Eventually Pawel found an old crate and turned it over to use as a mounting block.

"I hope you don't mind, Donut. Please say if you do," Kizzy said seriously to the pony.

Her next attempt was more successful. She leaned forward on the pony's back and pressed her weight against him. Donut didn't move. Kizzy took a handful of mane in one hand and swung her leg up and over. It was more of an undignified scramble than the smooth mount she'd pictured, but Kizzy was on her pony.

Ali and Lopa clapped. Donut shifted his weight and shook his mane out but otherwise seemed quite unbothered.

Kizzy sat with the biggest grin her face had ever worn. She felt amazing. She could feel the warmth of Donut's back and smell his delicious pony scent. She leaned forward and hugged him again from this new angle, burying her face in his scratchy, shaggy mane. "You're the best pony in the world. Thank you," she whispered.

"Look at you!" said Pawel, smiling at Kizzy proudly. "Want to walk now?"

Pawel had said she wouldn't be far off the ground on Donut, but that wasn't how it seemed to Kizzy now that she was up there. She felt like a mountaineer who'd reached the summit of Everest. Kizzy steadied herself. If she and Donut were eventually going to be jumping fences or doing championship dressage, they had better get started.

"OK," she said. "Walk on, Donut."

Kizzy tried to give the correct aids as memorized from her copy of *Correct Horsemanship for the Young Rider* by P. A. Pickford. It was a book she'd found at a yard sale and read so many times it was now puffy with tape repairs. According to P. A. Pickford, one needed to release the reins a fraction and give a gentle squeeze with the lower legs to instruct a horse to walk. Not having any reins to release, Kizzy focused on the second part, but her lower legs couldn't find any horse to squeeze. Donut might or might not have been tall, depending on your perspective, but from anyone's point of view he was wide. Kizzy's legs went out a long way before they went down at all, leaving her calves flapping hopelessly more or less in thin air. She tried to "sit tall and deep" and "keep in constant communication with the steed," but it wasn't as easy as P. A. Pickford made it sound.

Pawel said, "Come on, horse. Giddyup."

Donut swished away a fly with his tail and flicked his ears forward and back in an interested way, but didn't take so much as a single step.

"Maybe squeeze a bit harder," suggested Pawel, tugging the rope a little.

Kizzy finally managed to make some contact with Donut's sides and tried to press her heels in.

Still nothing.

"Come on, Donut. Walk!" In desperation, Kizzy gave a real kick to Donut's side. Pawel dug in and really pulled. Donut snorted in a resigned way and shuffled off.

"Hooray!" cheered Ali and Lopa.

Now Kizzy faced the new problem of trying to stay on. Donut's back was as slippery as his sides. She found herself sliding sideways, coming dangerously close to continuing all the way down and off. Curling her fingers in a section of mane for security, she tried to shift upright and look between Donut's ears. After a short distance, Kizzy started to get her balance.

They made a steady circuit of the gas tank imprint.

With perfect timing the sun came out from behind a cloud; the soft light made Donut's caramel-colored mane glow like he was in a shampoo ad. Kizzy might not have felt the wind in her hair, but she felt a gentle breeze on her face and the comforting rhythm of Donut's muscles working underneath her.

She was riding—actually riding—her pony! She wanted to sing and shout, to explode with joy; only that might have startled Donut. Kizzy settled for a quietly thrilled stroke of his neck.

Donut shared the thrill. He lifted his tail and marked the circle they plodded with a new trail of poop.

CHAPTER FIVE

"I've found a stray. I'd like to file a report, please."

Having been distracted by her ride and then forced to gallop to city hall on her own two legs, Kizzy had finally reached the front of the line just before the offices were due to close. The atmosphere was bad. Most people were waiting to argue about parking tickets and tax bills, clutching piles of paper and muttering under their breath. Kizzy, wrapped up in her own sadness, hardly noticed. She knew turning Donut in was the right thing to do, but now that she'd ridden him, giving him up was even harder. Her legs ached from where they'd been stretched around Donut's sides, and Kizzy wanted that ache never to go away.

"That makes a nice change!" The clerk gave Kizzy a tired smile from behind her glass booth and went rummaging under her desk for the file of lost and found animals. "Where is the animal currently? Are you happy to take care of them or do you want to bring them to the animal shelter? The animal control officer won't pick them up until Monday now, I'm afraid."

"It's fine. He's being taken care of by my friends. I don't think the animal shelter would be the right place for him anyway," said Kizzy.

"Poor boy. Nervous, is he?" The clerk paused and looked up, sympathetic.

"I wouldn't call him nervous, exactly . . ." Kizzy thought about Donut. "He mostly just likes to eat."

"Ah. Probably has some Labrador in him." The clerk nodded wisely. She suddenly brightened up. "I've got one." She picked up a photo on her desk and turned it to show Kizzy. "That's my Barbara. Ooh, she's a terror! She stole a kid's ice cream in the park the other day, right out of his hand! It was so embarrassing, I almost ran away." The clerk chuckled at the memory. "The kid was crying and his mom was yelling

at me. You had to laugh."
She gave the photo a
fond kiss.

The line of people
still waiting began to shift
and mutter more loudly.
Someone coughed point-
edly. The clerk wiped her
photo and returned to her desk.
"All right then, where and
when did you find him?"

"In the supermarket on Heatherington Road,
yesterday afternoon," said Kizzy, and the clerk wrote it
down. That one was easy.

"And description or breed of the animal?"

"He's brown and shaggy . . ." Kizzy took a deep
breath. "And he's a pony." She got it out in a rush.

The clerk, still writing in her ledger, chuckled
again. "Big dog, is he? That figures, with the appe-
tite. Reminds me of my aunt—now she didn't like
Labradors. She used to breed wolfhounds. Won prizes
with them. When I was a kid I used to try to climb on

their backs and ride them like they really were horses! I remember one afternoon—"

The person behind Kizzy in the line started rapping his stack of papers noisily against the side counter. The clerk stopped her story to frown at the man. "None of that, sir. You wait your turn." She turned back to Kizzy. "Another time, or we'll be here all day! Your fault for getting me started on dogs! Now then, what you must do next is take him to the vet and get him scanned to see if he has a microchip. That should have the owner's details. In the meantime, I'll make sure he goes in the database. You don't have a photo, do you?"

Kizzy shook her head. "But you don't understand; he's not a—"

The clerk kept talking. "Never mind. If you don't find his owner soon, bring him to the animal shelter or call the animal control officer after the weekend and we'll take care of him. OK, dear? Nice to chat to you! And the rest of you come back on Monday. We're closed."

And she slammed down the shutter of her booth.

* * *

Hurrying back, Kizzy found no sign of Donut or Pawel and his sisters where she'd left them. She walked through the underpass and into the park. It was very busy there now. Kizzy saw a group of people in tracksuits and Lycra being shouted at by a man with a whistle, and a few wobbly children learning how to ride their bikes. But she didn't see her pony anywhere.

She started to panic. Where could Pawel have taken him? Had he lost him? She wished she'd taken Donut to the city hall with her. Then the lady would have known for certain what sort of animal Kizzy was talking about.

Kizzy headed for the playground. It was heaving with small children, and she could see that an unusually large number of them were squeezed onto the merry-go-round. She quickened her pace.

She saw a flash of chestnut. She ran.

Donut's lead rope was tied to one of the metal arms of the merry-go-round. Ali and Lopa were taking turns finding handfuls of thick grass and dangling it just ahead of Donut, so that he had to keep walking in a big circle if he wanted the prize. As he moved he pulled the rope, keeping the merry-go-round and all of the children riding on it spinning. There were at least twenty of them on board. They were laughing and clapping and singing "Horsey, horsey, don't you stop!" in a chorus.

"I said to stay where I left you! What happened?" Kizzy said breathlessly when she reached Pawel. He was squeezed uncomfortably in the middle of a bench, sandwiched between three mothers chatting and a dad reading a newspaper.

Pawel looked up from his phone guiltily. "Yeah. Sorry. You took forever and the twins got bored, so I thought it would be all right to come back here. He's been no trouble. I said we'd rented him for a birthday party when anyone asked." He waved his hand at the merry-go-round. "They've been doing this for at least half an hour."

"This is pony abuse! Poor Donut," said Kizzy, rushing to untie him. There was a collective groan, both from the children who had lost their helpful puller and from the parents who were now going to have to take over.

"No, go away; he's had enough. He needs space," Kizzy said sternly as several three-year-olds came wobbling over and tried to pat Donut with sticky, snotty hands. Donut turned to accept a rice cake from one before Kizzy led him away to a quieter area. Here he could help himself to the grass without effort and without the risk of also eating a child's fingers. Pawel and the twins joined them.

"Sorry, Kizzy," said Ali.

"Would Donut like to try the zip line with us?" asked Lopa hopefully. "He could bring it back for the next person's turn."

"No! Go and play by yourselves," said Kizzy.

"So where did the city say we should take him? Has his owner been looking for him?" asked Pawel as the twins ran off.

"They said we should keep him for now. They haven't had anyone asking for him," Kizzy answered selectively. She didn't mention the misunderstanding. "I've been thinking—we don't know whether Donut wanted to escape from his old owners. What if we've rescued him from a life of cruelty? Maybe we need to protect him. What if his owner's planning to sell him for burger meat or something?"

"Ha! You could make a lot of burgers out of him."

"Pawel!"

"But if the city won't take him, what now? You're not planning to keep him in your bedroom, are you?"

"Yes," said Kizzy.

"Kizz, your mom's home. And Jem."

"Yes," said Kizzy in a smaller, sadder voice. She hugged Donut. If only ponies came with handy invisibility cloaks.

Pawel watched her and the pony thoughtfully. Then he called Ali and Lopa off the jungle gym. "Time to go home. We need to say goodbye to Mom and Dad and Marek."

"Oh, hooray!" cheered Lopa. "GranPam's coming to babysit us!"

"Mom and Dad are going over to Poland for the

week to show Marek off to Dziadek and Babcia," Pawel explained to Kizzy.

Kizzy stroked the warm hollow on the underside of Donut's jaw. It was soft and silky. "Is Marek getting any less screamy?"

"No." Pawel shrugged. "I guess it's hard being a baby. Anyway, Kizz, while they're away, I'm wondering—although obviously your bedroom is the perfect place for a pony, would you like a different place to keep Donut for a little while?"

CHAPTER SIX

"They've left! It's safe to come in now." Ali flung open the gate of the Kozlows' backyard and beckoned Kizzy and Donut in from where they were skulking by the trash cans in the alley. Marek's cries could be heard growing fainter down the road as the Kozlow parents' car drove away. "GranPam's in the living room with the TV on loud. She's ironing."

Pawel and Lopa appeared, too. "I love GranPam. She makes cake and lets us stay up late," said Lopa.

"Are you sure this is going to work?" Kizzy asked Pawel.

"No, but it's more likely to than your bedroom," said Pawel, patting Donut.

The Kozlows' shed was going to be Donut's new home, but first it needed to be cleaned out. Pawel, Ali, and Lopa's small bedroom became even smaller as they tiptoed up and down the stairs finding temporary homes for power tools, a pop-up soccer goal, rakes, shovels, and a lawn mower. Kizzy agreed to take two giant cans of paint home with her. Then they brushed the wooden walls clean of cobwebs, hosed down the concrete floor, and filled a bucket with water.

The shed looked satisfyingly stable-like when they had finished. Donut went in without complaint and stuck his nose out the hinged window. Ali and Lopa fed him Cheerios from their outstretched palms through the gap.

"What if the neighbors tell your parents? And won't GranPam see him from the kitchen?" Kizzy said, fretting.

"We'll hang sheets and towels on the clothesline to keep him out of view," Pawel replied reassuringly. "Anyway, I bet his owners will turn up long before Mom and Dad get back."

On the way home Kizzy bought more rabbit bales of hay, thanks to a loan from Pawel. He was the best

best friend, even if he didn't completely understand about horses yet.

The man at the pet shop was surprised to see her back. "Already got through the last bale? What sort of rabbit are you keeping?"

"A giant one. And she had babies . . ."

Lugging the paint cans and bags of hay, Kizzy was caught up with thoughts of everything else she needed to get for Donut as she let herself into the apartment.

"Kizzy? Can you come into your room, please?"

Kizzy's happiness evaporated at hearing her mom's most businesslike, telling-off voice. She must have found out. Kizzy felt sick: everything was over. She went into her bedroom and found her mom sitting on her bed, surveying the scene of disarray.

"I think it's time we had a talk, don't you?" Her mom patted the bed beside her. Kizzy sat.

"I'm sorry, Mom. I should have told you—"

Her mom put an arm round Kizzy and interrupted. She looked very serious. "I know growing up happens earlier and earlier these days, but it made me so sad to see this, Kizzy. You've torn up your horse poster and put away all your china ponies! I thought you loved them. Was it Jem and me teasing you? Or has someone been saying something mean at school? And why the tarp? Oh no. Of course." She caught sight of what Kizzy was holding. "Planning to repaint your lavender walls black, I guess? What's in the bag— makeup, high heels, and perfume? Oh, I'm not ready to lose my little girl!"

Kizzy's mom looked like she might cry.

Kizzy felt dizzy with relief. She hugged her mom tightly. "Mom, stop being embarrassing. You won't lose me. Don't worry. I was just . . . rearranging things. Experimenting with a different layout. That's OK, isn't it? I was going to put things back today."

Over her mom's shoulder Kizzy caught sight of the hay net dangling with a few strands still left inside. She reached out to knock it on the floor.

Her mom pulled away looking a little happier, then frowned. "And that's another thing! Where have you been all day? What with you not finishing your sandwich and then going for a run at dawn . . . Well, I've read about the pressure you girls are all under now, and I worry. Don't be in a hurry to grow up, Kizz. Stay true to yourself."

"Oh, Mom, don't be so dramatic! I will, I promise. I'm starving now; are there are any sandwiches left?"

Donut had been grazing all day; Kizzy hadn't been so lucky.

"Of course not. We live with Jem, don't we? And"— her mom raised an eyebrow—"there doesn't seem to be any milk or pasta, either. What happened to the money I gave you?"

Kizzy looked at her feet. "There was sort of an emergency. I'm sorry. I'll pay you back."

"Hmm." Her mom stood up. "Lucky for you I've been to the grocery store and stocked up, so you can make *yourself* another sandwich. Hey, you'll never guess what happened. Apparently they had a horse wandering around in there yesterday! Can you believe it? They don't know where it came from. The checkout lady said they were going to call the police but then its owner came and took it away, cool as can be. I bet you wish you had gone shopping now, right?"

"Really? A horse in the grocery store? Amazing."

"I'm glad to hear you haven't grown out of ponies quite yet. I've always felt bad that we don't live in the right place or have the money for you to take lessons. It's not fair to you. I mean, I expect we could manage for you to have a few lessons; only then, if you wanted to continue . . ." Kizzy's mom looked worried.

"It's fine, Mom. Honestly it is. I understand."

Kizzy's mom hugged her and ruffled her hair, then stood up to leave. "Anyway, whether you're growing out of ponies or not, I do want you to clean this room up right now. Honestly, it looks like a stable!"

"Yes, Mom."

As if she'd ever grow out of ponies, thought Kizzy. She didn't feel good about lying, though. Her mom worked hard for her and Jem, but that made it all the more important not to bother her with things Kizzy could figure out herself. Like keeping a pony.

Kizzy got out a paper and pen and started writing down a list of what Donut would need.

For Donut

Hay
Saddle
Bridle
More hay
Brushes

Shoes
Blankets?
Stable
More hay

Kizzy put down her pen and sighed. What she really needed was money. Ponies, even (possibly, probably) temporary ponies, were expensive. She went to make herself a sandwich.

Jem was in the kitchen working his way methodically through an entire loaf of bread.

"Don't eat all of that! Leave some for me."

"You're not growing like I am, squirtle! I suppose I can spare you half a slice. . . ."

"More than that!" Kizzy dived at the loaf, her brother snatched it away, and they wrestled over it until Jem crammed a whole piece in his mouth and ate it while Kizzy punched and tickled him. She won two slices and started to butter them.

"I bumped into the old bat from upstairs on my way back from football," said Jem when his mouth was free to talk again.

"Miss Turney? Don't call her a bat. She's OK."

"No, she is a bat: a batso, batty. Honest. Because she stopped me by the elevator and said to tell you that she had something for your pony."

Kizzy froze, her knife in midair. "Oh, did she? That *is* weird. I wonder what she meant?"

"Nothing at all I expect," said Jem. "Don't suppose she even knows who you are. Cuckoo, see?"

"Yeah, I guess so."

After she'd eaten, Kizzy went down to the ground floor. Taking a deep breath, she knocked on Mr. Newman's door. His moods were never predictable, but she had promised.

"What do you want?"

Kizzy was relieved to see that Mr. Newman was fully dressed when he answered.

"I promised I'd help you clean—I know I'm late. Do you still want me to?" She had an ulterior motive, but he didn't need to know that yet.

Grudgingly, Mr. Newman gave her a mop and bucket and said she could wash down the path outside. Kizzy did the best job she could, aware that Mr. Newman's curtains were twitching as he kept an eye on her from his apartment.

After a while he joined her and began picking up litter with hinged tongs.

"Terrible, the things people throw down and expect others to pick up after them," he grumbled. "As if I don't have enough to do. Not to mention my bad back."

"It can't be easy," said Kizzy. "I'm sorry about your back." She paused. "Perhaps I could help you out regularly? I'm sort of looking to earn a little bit—"

"Oh, you want to be paid, do you? I thought this was all for school. Now I understand." Mr. Newman scowled.

"No, no! This *is* for school. I meant if you wanted more help. It was only a suggestion. I won't mention it again."

There was silence. Kizzy concentrated on scrubbing bits of chewing gum off the pavement with the side of her shoe.

"All right," said Mr. Newman eventually. "You come and help me with all the bending jobs for an hour after school every day. Perhaps I could find you a little bit of gold . . ." He winked. "If you make yourself useful."

"Oh yes, Mr. Newman. Thank you!"

A job! It wasn't much but it was something. A bit of gold sounded promising. Kizzy hoped it would be enough to keep up with Donut's hay demands at least.

She put away the cleaning things and took the elevator to the thirteenth floor. Three different groups of people got on and off this time; it was good Donut was safe at Pawel's.

Kizzy hovered outside Miss Turney's door for a moment, wondering what she'd find behind it, before ringing the bell.

"Hello, dear!" Miss Turney opened the door with

a much more welcoming smile than Mr. Newman had. "Your brother passed on my message, then? Such a tall young man! And where's your pony? I was hoping you'd bring him. Come in, come in! I'll show you what I've found for you."

Kizzy wanted to come in, but it wasn't as easy as Miss Turney made it sound. Her apartment was already full. The hallway had piles of books and papers and bags crammed with clothes and toys and junk. Kizzy stepped over and squeezed past it all politely. Through every doorway she passed as she followed the old lady to the kitchen, she could see more: old electrical equipment, a whole box of shoes, china ornaments, teetering towers of musty-looking magazines. It was a warren of stuff.

"Sorry it's a little messy," said Miss Turney, beaming. "I'm not good at getting rid of things. But that's just as well, because you never know when you might need something. Now, where did I put them?"

She looked around her kitchen. This room at least had some empty chairs and a small table free of clutter, where Miss Turney had left some teacups

and more cookies. Maybe she lived off tea and cookies.
Kizzy approved.

"Ah yes. Here we are."

Miss Turney picked up a pile of old towels from a chair to uncover the purest treasure: a small saddle and bridle! Cracked in places, dusty and in need of cleaning and conditioning, but actual, real leather tack. "There now. Could your pony use that? It's very old, I'm afraid—almost as old as me! It was Robbie's. I used to ride him with it, when he'd let me."

"Oh, Miss Turney, really? It's exactly what I need! Thank you! Thank you so much!" Kizzy couldn't believe it.

Miss Turney sat down. "Maybe I'll come and see you ride the feller one day. I'd like that. It would take me back. He'd bite sometimes, Robbie! Ran away with me, too—we both almost ended up in the canal. I loved him, though. We all love our ponies, don't we? Whatever they do."

CHAPTER SEVEN

"What have you done to him?"

Kizzy stood at the open door of the Kozlows' shed
the next morning staring at Donut. Ali was holding his
halter and Lopa had her arms around his neck.

"Doesn't he look great? We gave him a makeover!"
said Lopa proudly.

"I can see that," said Kizzy. She put down the saddle
and bridle she was holding and took the lead rope from
Ali. "Come on, Donut. Come away from those mean
girls."

Pawel started laughing as the pony emerged. "Oh!
Sorry, Kizz! They've been in with him for a while. I
didn't know."

"He likes it," protested Ali. "He got a package of fig bars while we did it. Lopa gave him all her best sparkly hair bands."

"How could you? He does not like it. It's totally undignified," said Kizzy.

Donut stood in the middle of the yard and blew out from his nostrils. Flakes of glitter tumbled to the grass. It was difficult to tell what he thought about his new look. He appeared to have spent the night in a Claire's accessories store. Both his shaggy butterscotch mane and tail had been braided in sections with a wide-ranging collection of ribbons, scrunchies, and small elastic bands. His coat had been dusted with glitter and was streaked with pink and blue where the girls had experimented with hair mascara. His hindquarters were plastered with a collection of Disney princess stickers. Kizzy started to pull these off angrily, making a ball of Cinderellas and Sleeping Beauties and Elsas in her hand.

"Aw, let him keep the Anna and Sven sticker at least! That was my best one," protested Lopa.

"Donut is a serious animal. He's not a toy. I didn't stay up half the night cleaning and polishing this tack with Mom's special anti-wrinkle cream to put it on a My Little Pony," Kizzy said fiercely. "Today is supposed to be about real riding with posting trot and exercises for my seat. I won't be able to leave him here if I can't trust you."

Ali and Lopa looked miserable.

"Let it go, Kizzy," said Pawel. "They were just having fun. When else are they going to have the chance to groom a pony? He'll probably be claimed by his owner today anyway. Any news about that?"

"No news," said Kizzy. She sighed and squinted again at the pony. It wasn't so bad; the girls had only been loving him. She supposed she had tried out a few ribbons of her own in his mane when he'd been with her. And her braids hadn't stayed in half as well or been nearly so neat.

"Sorry, I'm just jealous. I've missed him so much. I think we'd better take these things off before we head out, though. He doesn't exactly blend in as it is."

She unraveled the ribbons and pulled off the elastic bands. Donut's mane was wilder than ever after it was unbraided.

"Look at his hair! It's like when Mom puts in her volumizing mousse and curlers," said Lopa. "He's so glamorous—he should be a model."

"OK, Donut, should we see if your saddle fits?" said Kizzy. "I know it's not perfect for you to be borrowing an old one, but I'll make sure it doesn't rub or pinch, and the leather's nice and soft."

Kizzy took a thin cushion from one of the Kozlows' patio chairs and put it on Donut's back to add another layer of protection.

"Why did your neighbor have a saddle around?" asked Pawel.

"You should see her apartment. I think she's got everything."

Getting the tack on Donut took all eight of their hands. The bridle had so many buckles and straps that at first Kizzy mixed up the browband and the noseband and put it on upside down. With the help of YouTube, they straightened it out. Donut didn't seem to care. He took the bit without any trouble. He obviously knew the routine.

"That bit should be spotless; I cleaned it with Jem's electric toothbrush last night," Kizzy reassured him.

The saddle fit well until it came to doing up the girth underneath.

"I think he might need a bigger size," said Ali, ducking under Donut's stomach to pass the dangling strap to Lopa on the other side.

"Let me try," said Kizzy. She hauled at the buckle, trying to make it catch the lowest holes. Pawel helped, and between them they just managed to get it done up. "There!"

A call came from inside Pawel's house.

"Hellooo! Who wants pancakes for breakfast? Where are you all?"

The four of them looked at each other in panic.

"Don't worry, GranPam; we're coming in now," shouted Pawel. "We're out in the yard . . . um . . . gardening! Kizzy's here, too."

"Here already? Hello, Kizzy! I'll make a couple extras then."

"Don't worry! I was just leaving," called Kizzy. She started to lead Donut away.

"What are you doing? You can't take him without us!" whispered Pawel.

"I should bring that laundry in; I can't see anything out the window," GranPam continued.

"It's still wet—I think it rained during the night," Pawel yelled back. He pushed Ali and Lopa under the sheet toward the back door. "Go distract her," he hissed. "Look," he continued to Kizzy. "We can put Donut back in the shed for now. You should come in and eat breakfast before you ride him anyway. Trust me, GranPam's pancakes are worth staying for."

Kizzy thought for a moment. Pawel was right: she shouldn't ride on her own. She wasn't ready yet. "OK. Ten minutes," she agreed.

She put Donut back in the shed and took his tack off, which turned out to be much easier than putting it on. When she finished, she hurried after the others.

GranPam's pancakes were very much worth staying for: they had powdered sugar and strawberries on top. After three helpings and a polite chat about school, the Sunshine Café, and baby Marek's stomach troubles, Kizzy carried the plates to the sink and made frantic eyebrow signals at Pawel.

"Thanks, GranPam, that was great. Can we go to the park now?"

"Of course. Take your phone and come back when you're hungry. And you girls be good for your brother."

The four of them hurried back outside. And then stopped short. The shed door was swinging open.

There was no longer a pony inside.

"But I did the latch! I'm sure I did!" cried Kizzy, searching inside the small shed in case Donut was somehow hiding.

"He can't have gotten far," said Pawel, standing on his tiptoes to look over the fence. "Do you think he jumped?"

"Look! The back gate's open. This way!" said Ali.

They pushed through and looked left and right down the alley. There was no sign of a chestnut-colored pony.

Kizzy glanced down. "We can follow the glitter!"

There was a faint but definite sparkle on the ground, leading off to the right. They tracked it past garbage cans and back gates.

"Told you our makeover was good," said Lopa, a little smugly. She peeled off the Anna and Sven sticker that had been caught on a fence post. Beyond it, the trail stopped. Pawel pushed tentatively at the next gate. It swung open to reveal the yard behind—and Donut.

"Oh no!" said Pawel. "Of all the yards he could have picked . . ."

Donut looked very happy and as if he had picked this yard deliberately. All four of his feet were planted on the neatest, greenest patch of lawn Kizzy had ever seen, and he was grazing along a raised vegetable bed. It had probably been neat once, too, but Donut was taking care of that. He was pulling out lettuces and stripping pea plants and strawberries. Trails of greenery hung down from either side of his mouth, although they were disappearing into it as he sucked up mouthfuls of leaves and stalks as easily as spaghetti in sauce.

The pony was splattered with mud right up to his hocks. This, Kizzy could see, was because Donut had waded directly through the yard's small ornamental pond to get to the vegetable patch. A mess of weeds and mud had spilled out all over a paved path. There was also a knocked-over miniature windmill and an unfortunate fishing gnome who had been parted from his head.

"Donut! No! This is bad," said Kizzy, advancing slowly. Donut watched her with interest. He shook his mane out and dropped onto his knees.

"NO! Please!" begged Kizzy. Too late. Donut rolled blissfully on his back, flattening the grass, before pushing himself up and shaking his whole body.

"What? No!" cried another voice from the other end of the yard.

A man was standing at his back door, staring at them. He rubbed his eyes, looked again, and shouted more confidently, "NO! A horse! My garden! A horse in my yard? Vandals! Get out of here! No, stay there—I'm

calling the police!" He pulled his phone out of his pocket and came toward Kizzy and Donut. "I'm making a citizen's arrest. None of you move. Especially not him." The man pointed at Donut.

Donut leaned forward and took another mouthful of climbing pea.

"Oh, please don't!" said Kizzy. "He got loose some-how. We're so sorry. We'll help clean everything up."

"That's a season's work destroyed. My prize in the Hope Green Growers' Summer Show is gone. You can't clean up dreams, missy. And —" The man caught sight of the broken gnome and rushed to pick up the pieces, cradling them in his arms. "Bilbo Beardy! He broke Bilbo Beardy!"

Feeling desperate, Kizzy looked at the others. Pawel was staring at his feet and both Ali and Lopa had started to cry. Slowly they shuffled forward, put the windmill upright, and began to pick up what was left of the plants.

The gardener's anger subsided at the sight of the sniffing pair with their handfuls of plants. "I suppose . . ." he began in a more conciliatory tone.

Donut chose that moment to raise his tail. Poop balls dropped one by one right into the middle of the scuffed, flattened, and muddied lawn.

The man stared at the brown pyramid as it piled up. They all stared at it. It was mesmerizing. If it had been an exhibit in a modern art gallery, it might have won a prize. There was one final *phut* noise as the last ball fell. Donut lowered his tail.

Kizzy screwed up her eyes and winced, waiting for the gardener's fury to erupt again. She thought she might start to cry herself.

But the gardener did not start yelling. He set the broken gnome down and picked up a shovel. "I'll keep this," he said, shoveling the pile up and looking at Kizzy challengingly. "You owe me this."

"Please take it!" said Kizzy quickly.

The man cocked his head to one side and assessed the contents of his shovel.

"We could bring you more if you want," Kizzy ventured. She held her breath.

The gardener nodded. Unbelievably, miraculously, he actually seemed to like Donut's poop.

"Might be enough to give me the edge over Dave at number forty-three on the roses and leeks this year. Secret formula, so to speak. Not going to have access to quality manure like this, is he?"

"He is not," agreed Kizzy.

"All right. Deal. Clean up and go away now. Keep me supplied and I won't call the police this time."

"Oh, thank you, thank you very much!" said Kizzy.

"What are you kids doing with a pony anyway?" asked the man. "Who has a pony around here?"

Kizzy and Pawel looked at each other, but it was Lopa who stepped forward.

"He's not ours," she said, looking up at the man with wide blue eyes still glassy with tears. "He belongs to my class at school. It's our turn to take care of him this weekend. There's a list."

The man nodded, satisfied. "Used to be a hamster in my day," he said. "But that's progress for you."

CHAPTER EIGHT

"Imagine if Donut really could be our school pony. Everyone would love him."

At the old gas tank site again at last, Ali held Donut's head and patted his neck while Kizzy tried to tighten his girth. It was loose enough for Donut's saddle to slip every time Kizzy put her foot in the stirrup, but impossibly tight when she took her foot out and tried to adjust it.

"Stop blowing your stomach out, Donut!" Kizzy said, giving his stomach a nudge with her elbow to deflate it. Donut shifted irritably and planted his hoof firmly on her foot. "OW! Get off me!"

Kizzy's today-I-will-learn-rising-trot plan was not going as well as it had in her head. She shoved against the pony's solid brown side. He relented and moved his hoof. Hopping on her good foot, Kizzy took the chance to fasten the girth buckle securely. "There!" Kizzy put her throbbing foot in the stirrup and scrambled into the saddle. She was learning.

"There will be a school pony tomorrow," Kizzy declared from her elevated vantage point.

"What are you talking about?" asked Pawel.

"I can't leave him in your shed all day, can I? It wouldn't be fair. Plus I'm sure he managed to undo that latch himself—I know I locked it. He must have undone it with his teeth. We'll have to keep the window shut from now on."

"Hang on, never mind the latch. Taking care of him for the weekend was one thing, but next week is another. Even if they can't trace his owner we should probably hand him over to the city or someone, because—and I hate to break this to you, Kizzy—YOU CAN'T TAKE A PONY TO SCHOOL!"

"You're so negative, Pawel," Kizzy replied. "We've

taken good care of him so far, haven't we? Much better than any animal control officer would have, I'm sure. And I have to take a pony to school because I have to be there."

Kizzy made clicking noises and Donut moved forward. Riding was definitely easier with a saddle and reins.

"So you're going to chain him to the bike racks for the day, are you? Or are you planning to bring him to homeroom and PE? Or will you dress him up and tell everyone he's your visiting cousin?" Pawel started laughing.

"You're hilarious. No, I've got a much better plan."

"Is he squeezed inside your backpack then?" Pawel whispered to Kizzy as they sat at their table waiting for attendance to be called. "You must have taken him early. I was up at seven and you'd already left."

"It was early," admitted Kizzy, stifling a yawn. "I had to be sure that no one would be around when we got here. It was amazing when we rode through the park. It was all misty and quiet, like a movie."

"Your pants are covered in hair. Did you get him to trot this time?" asked Pawel.

"No," Kizzy said defensively. She brushed at her pants. It wouldn't be good if they got ruined as well as her skirt.

Yesterday's attempts to encourage Donut to go at any speed other than a slow walk had not been a success. He didn't respond to any of the aids that P. A. Pickford said he should in Kizzy's book. Either he hadn't read P. A. Pickford's book or Kizzy wasn't doing them right. Or both.

"I think he must be very tired. Maybe he's been working in mines or something terrible for years. We can stick to a walk; I'm fine with that."

"I don't think they have ponies in mines anymore. I don't think they even have mines," said Pawel. "So where is he now?"

"Pawel and Kizzy, this is not the time for chatting. You know the rules!" Mr. Wilson called from the corner.

"I'll show you at lunch," muttered Kizzy.

It was a very long morning. Kizzy stared out the window, on alert for shaggy brown shapes wandering

across the playground. She was almost sure everything would be OK. But try as she might to focus on
the lesson, labeling a diagram of the water cycle while
being exhausted and on horse watch was hard. She
doodled pictures of Donut's head in her cumulonimbus
cloud stack. Kizzy felt confident about drawing horses'
heads, but if she attempted anything below the neck,
they never looked right. Horse legs were impossible.
She wished she could just sit with Donut and a sketch
pad until she got the hang of it, and not worry about the
difference between evaporation and condensation.

When the lunch bell rang, she and Pawel walked
across the playground with their lunch boxes. "This
way—but, you know, act casual. We don't want to
attract attention."

At the back of the playground, past the concrete
rectangle where everyone played soccer, there was a
fence and a locked gate. Trees and bushes hung over,
screening the small space beyond.

"The wildlife garden? He's in there?"

"He's wildlife! Isn't it perfect? There's grass and
water and everything."

"How did you get him in there?" Pawel asked.

"Through the back gate on the other side of the garden," Kizzy replied. "The caretaker unlocks it outside school hours to allow local people to use it as part of their community hub thing. I think that angry lady with the bells and scarves who came and yelled at us to meditate last year does evening tai chi classes there. I'll take Donut out again when school is over."

"What if a class goes in there and finds him?"

"Pawel," Kizzy said seriously, "when do any of us ever go in the wildlife garden? We haven't been in since we drew tadpoles, and that was years ago. Mr. Wilson said 'Never again' after Georgia pushed Mohammed in the pond and Yasmin lost her bracelet in the worm bin."

"You've got a point."

"Donut! You OK in there? Want some apple?" Kizzy called quietly. She stood on her tiptoes and stuck her arm through the leaves with the fruit in her hand. She heard a rustling and then felt warm breath and hairy wet lips snuffling against her palm. It tickled and she giggled. Donut had obviously survived the morning. Kizzy craned to see him clearly, but the leaves provided too thick a screen.

"I'm going in. I need to give him a proper hug. Keep a lookout, will you, Pawel?"

"Kizzy, don't! You'll only attract attention and if you get caught, so does he . . ."

But Pawel was speaking to Kizzy's back. She was already trying to climb over the fence.

"And so do I!" he added. He accepted the inevitable and gave her a leg up.

Kizzy dangled and dropped down onto the ground on the other side of the fence. She pushed through the greenery into the clearing with the pond. Brambles snagged at her sweater and tangled in her hair. There was a crunching noise underfoot: the wildlife garden was growing wild over a layer of empty chip bags and raisin boxes that other kids had been throwing over the fence. Kizzy found Donut sniffing through the trash, vacuuming up long-forgotten crumbs, moldy sandwich crusts, and apple cores.

Kizzy's heart melted at the sight of his lovely toffee-colored face. His mane rippled down in soft waves over his neck, and his smooth, well-brushed coat glowed like polished amber. The sounds of the school playground and the traffic beyond retreated. All Kizzy could hear now was birdsong, insects humming, and Donut's rhythmic chomping.

She sat down on the small patch of grass and watched her pony. Time had stopped. It was just the two of them and this secret woodland glade. Here they might live forever, free from school and responsibility and at one with nature and the changing seasons. They would gallop across flower-strewn meadows by day and curl up by a campfire in a simple wooden shelter at night. Kizzy would sing with Donut by her side, and squirrels and rabbits and deer would come and listen. And she would weave useful things like baskets out of cattails, and they would eat berries and acorn bread and want for nothing because they had each other.

Overcome by the beauty of it all, Kizzy got up off the damp ground and buried her face in Donut's side.

He was so warm and good and wonderful. He smelled sweet and a little bit sweaty all at once.

Donut continued to eat scrubby bits of grass and pull at leaves. He nosed out the prize of a granola bar still half in its wrapper that looked as if it might have been there for several months and crunched down on it.

"Kizzy! Kizzy! The bell just rang. Come out of there! We've got to go to music."

Kizzy blinked at Pawel's voice hissing urgently from the other side of the fence. Donut was so lucky not to have music class. Who needed a class for music anyway? Nothing and nobody would make her sing sweeter songs than Donut. Reluctantly, she gave her pony one last hug and kiss.

"Be good. I'll see you in a couple of hours and we'll ride again. Maybe you'll feel like a trot then?" Donut didn't break off his grazing to answer. "It doesn't matter if you don't." Kizzy checked that his saddle and bridle were still where she had left them on an overhanging branch and turned back to the fence.

"Kizzy, I can't wait any longer. Mrs. Potter has seen

me and is doing her tapping her watch and beckoning thing. Come back NOW!" Pawel called again.

"You go ahead; I'm coming. Thanks for standing guard," Kizzy replied. She pushed through the brambles and went to climb back over the fence.

That was when Kizzy realized that the wildlife garden had been built in a hollow. The fence was higher on this side than where she'd climbed over from the playground, and there was nothing to get a solid foothold on without Pawel to help. Kizzy reached up and scrabbled against the posts but found herself sliding back down.

"Pawel! Pawel? Help! I can't get back up!" she cried.

There was no reply; Pawel had already gone. The quietness of the playground seemed ominous now. Kizzy was going to be late. She looked back at her pony. "Donut! You'll help me, won't you?"

Kizzy calculated that from Donut's back she would be able to grab the top of the fence, climb over, and drop down on the other side. All she needed was to get him close enough.

But without a saddle, mounting Donut was no

easier than mounting the fence. Kizzy tried to persuade him to move to a good spot. He wasn't interested in being helpful. She rummaged in her pockets. Right at the bottom of one she struck gold: a single fluff-covered extra-strong mint. It was lucky for her pants that Donut hadn't smelled it earlier.

Kizzy climbed onto one of the posts of the small jetty that jutted over the pond. Balancing precariously, she stretched out her palm with the treasure in the middle.

"Donut!" she called softly. "Come here, Donut!"

This time the pony's head came up. His nostrils widened, sniffing the air. Then he bundled toward her with enthusiasm—with quite urgent enthusiasm, in fact.

"Oh! OK, Donut—slow down!"

Kizzy realized her mistake and put her hand up to ward off the approaching stampede. It was too late; Donut was already snatching the sweet. As he barged into her, Kizzy first wobbled, then completely lost her balance.

She slipped backward off the jetty post—away from Donut, already chewing his mint safely on the bank—straight into the school wildlife pond.

CHAPTER NINE

"The good thing about you bursting in half-drowned stopped us from having to hear any more of Tianna's terrible rendition of 'Over the Rainbow' on her recorder," said Pawel after school.

They had just smuggled Donut through the Kozlows' back gate. GranPam had finally taken down the laundry, but she was safely in the living room helping the twins with homework. They hurried the pony into the shed.

"Although you did drip onto the glockenspiel and ruin my solo," Pawel continued. "What did Ms. Khan say?"

"I think she wanted to give me her full 'You've let yourself and me and all of us down' talk, but I was making a puddle on her office carpet, so she just gave me a warning and sent me away."

Kizzy gazed into Donut's deep brown eyes as he nosed his hay net and sighed. He was so gorgeous. It wasn't his fault. Well, it was a little his fault, but it didn't matter. She'd forgive him anything.

The important thing was that Donut had remained undiscovered. Miss Robert, the music teacher, had been too upset about the disruption to scrutinize Kizzy's story about losing track of time unblocking a sink in the girls' bathroom. And Kizzy and Donut had even almost trotted this afternoon—for a short, bumpy, perfect minute when Donut had seen Pawel up ahead eating a bag of chips.

She kissed the pony's nose and he whickered his lips in return. He might have been kissing her back, or he might have been retrieving a strand of hay stuck in her hair. Kizzy decided she would take it as a kiss.

"I've got to go. I need to drop this load at your neighbors." Kizzy held up the day's backpack of poop. "Then help Mr. Newman, do homework, and find something to wear to school tomorrow since my skirt's been eaten and my pants are drenched."

"Aren't you forgetting to add 'call the city to find out if they've located his owner'?" asked Pawel.

Kizzy ignored him.

"I hate leaving Donut, but I'll be back first thing in the morning," she said. "Don't forget to keep the shed window shut."

"We'll take care of him. We know all about ponies now. But, Kizzy," Pawel said, sounding serious, "this won't work for much longer. You know that, don't you?"

Kizzy did know it. She knew it as she walked slowly home, having emptied her bag onto the compost heap of the gardener down the alley. She knew it as she helped

Mr. Newman mop and pick up trash. She knew it as she pushed pasta spirals in tomato sauce around her plate, making little swirling patterns.

"You not eating that?" asked Jem hopefully.

"She is eating it. Hands off, Jem — eyes off, too. Don't even look at it. You've had plenty," said Kizzy's mom. "What's up, Kizz? I've barely seen you for days. What's the Kizzy-news report?"

"I got a warning from Ms. Khan," admitted Kizzy.

"You got sent to the principal? Hooray! Finally!" Jem was ecstatic. "What did you do? You never do anything."

"I'm disappointed to hear that, Kizzy." Her mom looked serious.

"I was late for music class. I'm sorry." Kizzy had a sudden thought. She forked pasta into her mouth as she spoke. "Mom, what are the rules on having animals in our building?"

"Don't change the subject," said her mom. "And don't start that again. You said you didn't want another gerbil after Nibbles died."

"I don't. But I wondered whether there were official rules about it."

"I'd have to look at the paperwork, but as far as I remember, you have to get permission for a dog or a cat. And it can't be dangerous or cause a nuisance."

"It's only dogs and cats that you need permission for?"

"Think so. We didn't need to for Nibbles anyway."

Jem interrupted the conversation with a noisy burp and pushed his chair away from the table.

"And luckily we don't have to get permission for nuisance teenage boys, either, or we'd be out on the street," finished Kizzy's mom, getting up and clearing the dishes.

Later, Kizzy lay on her bed and gazed at the tattered remains of her gray stallion poster. Donut wasn't going to be able to live in the Kozlows' shed for much longer, and what then? She and Donut might be able to share her bedroom, once Mom had met him and had understood their unbreakable connection. If there were no rules saying you couldn't keep a horse, who could complain? Mr. Newman would be OK once he saw how useful Donut was at keeping the grass trimmed and picking up trash. He wouldn't ever need to use the mower or sweep up food again.

Kizzy wondered how best to introduce Donut to Mom and Mr. Newman so that they could see the advantages of keeping him. She thought about how it usually happened in her books. The pony generally won a show-jumping medal, but occasionally they saved somebody from drowning or a fire or something. Kizzy had to admit that Donut winning a medal was still a ways off, despite today's progress on trotting. And although she was certain he would save her life in an emergency, Kizzy felt it would be better not to put Donut under any pressure.

If only she lived next door to an apple orchard or a convenient farm with empty stalls like most pony book children seemed to. Why couldn't whoever had built their building have added a pasture or a cross-country course? Even if it was just a small one. Jem and his friends had the soccer field, after all. It wasn't fair.

In her head, Kizzy heard Pawel's reasonable voice telling her that Donut wasn't hers at all—that the time had come for her to take him to the animal shelter, or to call the animal control officer and ask him to come and take him back to whatever stables he had come from. But the thought of never seeing Donut again was unbearable. She threw herself onto her stomach and buried her head under the pillow. She could continue to take it day by day, Kizzy decided. That was enough for now.

Kizzy's worries that Donut might be lonely or escape in the night were soothed when she tiptoed into the Kozlows' backyard the next morning. Unlatching the shed door, she found Ali and Lopa curled up in sleeping bags, squished in one corner beside a dozing Donut.

"Don't be mad, Kizzy," said Lopa, popping her head out from her bag. "We wanted to guard him for you. We shut the window once we'd bolted ourselves in."

"I'm not mad," said Kizzy. "But won't GranPam have noticed you were missing?"

"We waited until she was in bed to come out. Pawel was asleep, too. We were very brave," said Ali.

"Yes, we were—there were strange noises in the night and I thought there was a ghost coming to get us and I was going to scream, but then we figured out it was Donut's stomach rumbling." Lopa wriggled all the way out of her sleeping bag and inspected it. "Oh, bananas, he's chewed my sleeping bag! The stuffing's coming out."

"Can we help you this morning, Kizzy? Can we

come with you if we get dressed fast and bring all our school stuff?"

Kizzy looked at them and smiled. They had been brave. She felt jealous again; she couldn't imagine a better place to spend the night. "Yes, if Pawel says it's OK. In fact, do you want to ride? Bring your scooter helmets and wear your school shoes—not sneakers, because they're not safe to ride in."

The two girls hugged her. "Can we really? Yes, yes, yes, please!"

The sun had risen but was still low in the sky. The shadows it cast of the four children and the pony were stretched long and, in Donut's case, unusually thin as they walked slowly through the streets to the park. Early morning traffic, garbage trucks, and buses trundled past. Donut gave them the occasional curious glance but didn't alter his pace.

"Think how wonderful it would be if everyone went back to horses instead of cars. No pollution, no noise. Everyone would start their day happy from riding," said Kizzy.

"Not sure about that," said Pawel. "When we

learned about the Victorian times, do you remember Mrs. Butcher telling us that horse manure was piled everywhere then? People were worried their houses would get completely buried under it. The city stank."

"I think horse manure is a nice smell—sort of warm and comforting," said Kizzy.

"Ew, Kizzy! Are you going to start a business selling eau de poop perfume and scented candles? I'm not investing. Count me out."

"But I bet the Victorians grew gorgeous roses and leeks." Kizzy led Donut through the park gates. She turned to Ali and Lopa. "OK, who's first?"

"Me!" cried the girls in unison.

After tossing a coin, Kizzy and Pawel lifted Lopa first and then Ali onto Donut's back and led each of them around in a small circle. The twins beamed.

Kizzy was about to get on for her turn when she had a thought. "What about you, Pawel?"

Pawel put his hands up. "No, no. I'm keeping my feet on the ground, thanks."

"Oh, come on, Pawel! You a scaredy-cat? Frightened of Donut? We've done it," said Ali.

"I'm not scared; I'm just not made for riding. I'm a city boy; I ride on bikes and buses and the subway."

"But Donut is a city pony now," Kizzy said. "You've definitely got to try it. No excuses—you can use my helmet."

Kizzy, Ali, and Lopa all stared hard at Pawel as Kizzy held out her bike helmet and waited. There was a brief standoff.

"Oh, OK then. A very short ride and that's all."

It was Kizzy's turn to give a leg up. Pawel looked over both shoulders to make sure no one was watching before launching himself into the saddle like someone leaping out of a plane uncertain their parachute would work.

"Whoa! Steady there!" he squeaked. It was unnecessary; as usual Donut wasn't going anywhere.

"How do you feel? Do you like it?" asked Lopa.

"Weird." Pawel straightened himself nervously. "Yeah, it's good, I guess. He's bigger than you think, isn't he?"

Kizzy made a clicking noise and Donut walked forward.

"Hey, I'm a cowboy! No, wait—I'm the sheriff," said Pawel. "Guess it's jus' me and my good ol' hoss, and we gonna keep the badlands free of trouble," he drawled, taking his feet out of the stirrups and holding the reins in one hand.

Which was exactly the moment that trouble arrived.

CHAPTER TEN

The Chihuahuas came from nowhere. Two tiny, pointy-eared, bulgy-eyed, yapping, nipping bombs who dashed in between Donut's feet in outrage at finding an interloper on their territory. One of the dogs was wearing a tiny pink tutu, and the other was dressed in a studded leather bomber jacket.

And Sheriff Pawel's horse, who hadn't been bothered by anything so far, was definitely bothered by the arrival of these Wild West outlaws. His tail immediately clamped down and his ears went back. He jerked his head up, pulling the lead rope from Kizzy's hands. He sidestepped and kicked out.

"Whoa!" said Pawel, tipping forward and grabbing a handful of mane.

The Chihuahuas continued barking and snapped at Donut's fetlocks. Kizzy tried, unsuccessfully, to get a hold of their sparkly collars. She looked for an owner; the only person she could see was a woman in a powder-blue velour tracksuit on a park bench. She had her back to them. Kizzy could see she was busy flicking through screens on her cell phone.

"Hello! Help! Are these your dogs?" Kizzy called.

Donut had bunched himself up and was baring his teeth at the Chihuahuas.

"Have my darlings done their morning poopsies? I'll come with a baggie." The woman turned around and looked up from her phone. Her jaw dropped. "OMG! Is that a horse? Don't you go near my angels! Elvis and Marilyn, come back to Mommy!"

But the angels were not listening to their mommy, and Donut had had enough. As Kizzy watched, helpless, the dog in the bomber jacket tried to sink his teeth into Donut's leg. Donut kicked out, sending the thwarted Chihuahua tumbling away.

The woman in the tracksuit screamed. The dog got back to his feet and yapped louder than ever. And for the first time, without Pawel needing to give any aids at all, Donut shot off, racing away across the open grass.

"He can canter! He can gallop! Oh, it's not fair. Why should Pawel have all the fun?" said Kizzy in admiration—which quickly changed to panic. "But can he stop? Hold on, Pawel. HOLD ON!"

Donut was heading for the cover of the trees at the other end of the park. Kizzy, Ali, and Lopa took off after the disappearing brown bottom as fast as they could.

"Stop right there! What's he done to my poor babies? I'm reporting you to the police!" called the woman, picking up her dogs and loading them into a customized handbag decorated with an E and M in rhinestones. She didn't join the chase but had her phone up and was filming them.

Kizzy could see Pawel bouncing around in the saddle on the bolting Donut. He looked like a rabbit trying to hold on to a pogo stick. As she watched, slowly, inevitably, the Pawel-rabbit started to lose the little balance he'd started with. As the pair reached the trees, Pawel ducked to avoid being hit in the face by a branch. Kizzy saw him try to sit up again, bounce over to one side, and then, in slow motion, keep sliding around. There was no possibility of recovery. Pawel hit the ground and rolled away. Donut kept on running.

"Pawel! Are you OK?" Kizzy raced over to her friend, all out of breath.

"I think I'm still in one piece." Pawel sat up looking dazed, rubbed his arms, and checked himself over. "Nothing broken. But I tell you what, Kizz: I am never getting on a horse again. Strictly bikes from now on. Bikes have brakes."

"Oh, Pawel, I'm sorry. Those stupid dogs and their even stupider owner. Who'd have thought they'd be the launch button for Donut?" Kizzy helped her friend to his feet. "And—Oh no. Where's he gone?" Kizzy scanned the horizon, feeling a sick lump in her throat and the prickle of tears. "He disappeared. He completely disappeared."

"That's probably how his real owner lost him," said Lopa, not altogether helpfully.

"He'll have run into the road and the traffic and been squashed by a car and broken his leg on his reins and gotten lost and I'll never see him again and he'll be dead and it'll all be my fault," said Kizzy. The tears started to flow.

"Not all those things at once," said Pawel. He gave Kizzy a brisk hug. "This is Donut we're talking about. He'll be near food, won't he? We'll find him. Come on, let's get on the trail. We've still got time before school."

With only a slight limp and wince, Pawel marched forward with the twins close behind him.

"School! Who cares about school?" wailed Kizzy, following. "I should never have taken him from the grocery store. I should have let the city take him — should have made them understand. I'm not fit to be a horse owner. This has all been a stupid idea. I'm nothing but an irresponsible thief. I stole a pony and then I killed him."

"You know what I think," said Pawel. "But go easy on yourself, Kizz; it was those dogs' fault. You've taken good care of Donut — and look!"

As they turned the corner to leave the park, there, sides heaving, was Donut. He was nuzzling Miss Turney. She held his bridle and stroked his broad nose.

"Lost someone, did you?" Miss Turney smiled at Kizzy. "Met this feller at the gate. He remembers my cookies, don't you, boy? Ah, he's just like my Robbie was, just the same. And I see Robbie's saddle fits him perfectly. You've polished it up nicely."

Kizzy saw that Miss Turney had her slippers and pajamas on under her coat. But she didn't care what her neighbor was wearing: she'd saved Donut. Kizzy ran to them both and threw her arms first around the pony and then Miss Turney.

"Thank you, oh, thank you so much — for the tack and even more for this. He got frightened by some dogs and bolted. I wasn't sure he could go faster than a walk; he'd never done it before."

"Ponies make their own decisions about when to go fast or slow," agreed Miss Turney. "I forget some things now, but I remember that very clearly."

Kizzy ran her hands down Donut's legs to check for lumps or swellings. She didn't really know what she was doing, but she'd seen vets do it in movies and it looked professional. Nothing seemed to be amiss, which was to say that Donut's legs had the same lumps they'd had the last time she felt them. She checked particularly carefully around the ankle that the Chihuahua had attacked. There were no puncture wounds or signs of bleeding. The thick, tufted hair covering Donut's fetlocks had protected him well. She relaxed and hugged him again.

"We'd better get going if we want to take Donut to

the animal shelter before school," said Pawel. "I need to drop the twins off, too."

"Oh, I don't think we should take him this morning. There's no hurry," said Kizzy.

"But you were just saying—"

"He's OK. We're OK. And Donut likes it in the wildlife garden. It'll be fine for today. Besides"—Kizzy patted the pony's neck and smiled at her friend—"now that I know he can canter that beautifully, I want to try myself. Then we'll find his owner."

Kizzy turned away from Pawel and mumbled into Donut's mane, "If that owner even exists." She felt hope and plans bubbling once more.

"He's a lovely-looking feller. There should be more ponies and horses, like the old days," mused Miss Turney. She produced yet another cookie from her pocket, which disappeared into Donut.

"Exactly. There should be. And we can start with one," said Kizzy. She looked again at Miss Turney. Weren't pajamas and slippers the most comfortable clothes anyway? When she was a grown-up, maybe she wouldn't bother changing out of them, either. Saying goodbye to Miss Turney, she took Donut past Pawel and into the alley that led to the wildlife garden.

Despite his morning, Donut showed no interest in cantering or even trotting at the old gas tank site that afternoon. Kizzy gathered up the reins and tried to urge him forward.

"Do you want me to pretend to be a Chihuahua? I could go on all fours and yap," offered Pawel.

"No!" said Kizzy, giving up. "Poor Donut's

probably still traumatized and tired out from this morning. I shouldn't put him under pressure. It's just that I've always dreamed of cantering—I can't believe you got to do it on your first ride."

"I didn't enjoy it much. I can't recommend it," said Pawel.

"You weren't prepared, that's all. 'A good rider should stay in control at all times and let the horse know who is master.' That's what P. A. Pickford says."

"I know you like that book, but P. A. Pickford hasn't been right about much so far, has she? Or are they a he?"

"They're a she. There's a photo at the front of her in a riding jacket with a hairnet on. She looks kind of fierce. You wouldn't mess with her."

"Maybe you should try wearing a hairnet," suggested Pawel.

Kizzy drew herself up with dignity. "Donut will canter with me because he loves me and wants to, not because I force him." She sighed. "Or at least I hope he will. Eventually."

CHAPTER ELEVEN

"Do you have any pets? Do you like animals?" Kizzy asked Mr. Newman as they rubbed at graffiti in the elevator with rags and cleaning spray. It couldn't hurt to test the waters about moving Donut in. Kizzy tried not to think about the look Pawel would give her if he were there.

"I hate them. Hate their smell and noises and messes—dog poop is the worst. Those who don't clean up their dog poop should have their noses rubbed in it and be kicked out by the housing association," said Mr. Newman, sounding even more cranky than he usually did.

"Oh," said Kizzy. She kept on scrubbing, discouraged.

They worked in silence for a while. A black heart with "T 4 J 4 EVR" inside it was slowly fading away.

"However," offered Mr. Newman, several minutes later, "there is one animal I like. One I'm happy to have here even though most people think they don't belong in the city."

"Oh yes?" said Kizzy, hope swelling. "I don't think being in the city should stop anyone from keeping an animal if they can take care of it."

Mr. Newman put down his rag. "I wasn't expecting you'd keep at this. You're like me." He smiled at Kizzy a little shyly. "So maybe you'd like to meet my animals? You can't tell anyone else about them, though. I can't have everyone going up there to see them."

"Sure, I can keep a secret!" said Kizzy. She felt excited. Had some friends for Donut been living here all along?

"Press the button for the top floor then."

On the twentieth floor, Mr. Newman beckoned Kizzy to the stairwell. He led her up a final flight of stairs that she'd never been up before. There was a locked door at the top with a sign marked AUTHORIZED PERSONNEL ONLY.

"The roof? Jem will be jealous. He's always wanted to come up here."

"Which is why I always keep the door locked. It's not a place for teenagers to hang out," said Mr. Newman, taking out a bunch of keys from his pocket. He unlocked the door and pushed it open. "Be careful."

Kizzy took a deep breath, butterflies in her stomach. Maybe it was going to be like *The Secret Garden.* Perhaps she'd find a paddock on the other side. Maybe the whole roof of the building had been seeded for grass and Mr. Newman kept a miniature Shetland or even a tiny Falabella.

As she stepped out, she found the roof disappointingly gray and concrete. She could see satellite dishes, cables, large metal tanks, and a big humming fan unit, but there definitely wasn't a horse. Of course there wasn't a horse. Kizzy sighed.

"I don't see any animals."

"This way," Mr. Newman said. "Quiet now."

He led Kizzy to the other side of the roof. There was a large, unremarkable-looking wooden box. She hadn't noticed it among all the other roof fixtures. "There are forty thousand animals in that. Can you hear them?"

"Bees!" said Kizzy. She could see little brown-and-yellow striped bodies flying in and out of a slot near the top of the box, enjoying the late-afternoon sun. They buzzed out through the railings at the edge of the roof and then ducked down out of sight. As Mr. Newman had suggested, she could hear them, too. She crouched down and listened. The whole box hummed and vibrated with its own secret music. It wasn't a pony, but it was a little bit magical.

"Are there really forty thousand of them?" she asked.

"Give or take. I haven't counted."

Kizzy stood up and looked around. "But what do they eat? It's all buildings here. Don't they need fields and flowers?"

"Actually, it's like a buffet out there for them. City bees can choose from all the little gardens and parks. And they can find it all from up here; they fly down and visit the window boxes and balconies and tree blossoms on the way. Their honey tastes even better for it."

Kizzy looked out over the roof railings. The view from her own bedroom was good, but from here she could see so much more that it was dizzying. Mr. Newman was right. She'd always thought she lived somewhere mostly gray and brown, ordered in rows of concrete and brick. From up here it looked much more wild. There were little patches of green everywhere, as well as the larger expanses of parks and playgrounds. And there were so many more bushes and trees than she'd thought— almost as many canopies of leaves as there were roofs, in fact. Why shouldn't bees be happy here? And if they were, why shouldn't ponies be, too? Donut certainly enjoyed all the different food options available to him. Maybe this was a better home for him than his old one.

But Kizzy then looked farther, much farther, to the horizon, where the buildings were lower and more widely spaced. She could see the point where they stopped altogether—the actual edge of the city. A strip of green lit up by the late-afternoon sun like a promised land. Maybe fields like those were where Donut had come from, fields that looked to be within touching distance but were really miles away, filled with ponies and horses and stables and kids who could ride well and knew how to canter.

"These bees are workers, see. Like you and me," said Mr. Newman, opening the door to the stairwell and ushering Kizzy back inside. "Another day you can help me gather honey, but we need special outfits for that."

"Thank you, I'd like that," said Kizzy politely. She wasn't really sure she had time to take care of another forty thousand unpredictable animals along with the one she already had. And, however much he seemed to approve of her, Kizzy had to admit it was unlikely Mr. Newman would want a pony sharing his bees' roof.

"I've got something for you: your first payment.

You've earned it." Mr. Newman reached into his pocket.

"Really?" Kizzy tried not to sound too eager. How much would it be? She just needed enough to get another bag or two of hay. And if there was anything left over, she'd be able to start saving for new shoes for Donut. Or maybe a blanket for the winter—a royal blue one would look nice against his coat, with red trim and his name embroidered in one corner . . .

"Promised you gold, didn't I? There you go—more where that came from. Best gold there is."

"Oh. Thank you." Kizzy looked down at the shining jar of honey Mr. Newman had given her. It wasn't going to buy a royal blue blanket or a set of horseshoes. It wasn't even going to buy the next bag of hay. She felt her face flushing red.

Mr. Newman didn't notice. "Same time tomorrow?" He summoned the elevator.

"Sure," Kizzy managed before waving and taking the stairs two at a time back to the twelfth floor. She dumped the honey on the kitchen table and continued to the safety of her bedroom. She threw herself flat on her bed and thumped the mattress in frustration. It wasn't fair. It just wasn't fair.

"Kizzy! Wake up." Kizzy's mom was shaking her shoulder. "Asleep at this time? What's wrong? Come and have some dinner."

"Donut?" said Kizzy groggily. She'd been having a dream where her pony had sprouted wings and she was flying him across the city, buzzing down into flowers and then watching him poop out small jars of honey in a stable full of other striped ponies.

"That would be nice. I haven't got any, though. We could make some tomorrow with that honey that's appeared, if your brother's left any," said her mom, stroking her hair.

"That's my wages!" said Kizzy, sitting up.

"He only had a taste. I've made enough beans and baked potatoes to fill even Jem's hollow legs. And what do you mean, 'wages'? How come you've got honey?"

"Mr. Newman gave it to me. I've been helping him. I thought he was going to pay me money, but turns out that's what he meant."

"Did he? But why honey? I feel so out of touch. Is it working for him that's making you fall asleep before you've even had your dinner? I don't like seeing you this tired, Kizzy. You're out so early each morning and then back late. And why do you need money anyway? Come and eat and tell me what's going on."

Kizzy followed her mom into the kitchen, where Jem was already helping himself to a second potato. She carefully selected which of her mom's questions to answer. "It's Mr. Newman's own honey. He makes it.

Or his bees do. Don't tell anyone, but he keeps them up on the roof."

"Really?" Kizzy's mom was successfully distracted. "I didn't know you could do that. What do they eat up there?"

"Nothing on the roof, but they can find all the flowers and gardens from there. Mr. Newman showed me. You wouldn't believe how green it is around here when you look down on it, Mom."

"He took you up there? I hope it's safe."

"Bees on the roof? Freaky! What if they're mutant killer bees and they swarm down and attack?" Jem jabbed at Kizzy with his potatoey fork and made a face. Kizzy ignored him.

"Anyway." Kizzy's mom got back on track. "I'm glad you've been helping him, but that can't be the whole story for why you're exhausted. What about all these early mornings of yours?"

"I'm not exhausted. I can manage. I've been helping Pawel with the twins, that's all. You know his parents are in Poland this week," said Kizzy, trying not to let a yawn out.

"OK," said her mom. She paused and looked at Kizzy appraisingly. "How about this Saturday you and I have one of our special days out? We haven't done that in forever. We can go shopping together, go to the movies, and have a burger somewhere. I think you could use some new shoes."

"Bring me back a shake and fries," said Jem.

Kizzy tried to find the right thing to say that would disguise the horror she felt—the very idea of losing a whole precious Saturday with Donut! A day that could be spent grooming him, loving him, learning to canter, even building a jump. She had thought of so many plans for Saturday already, and none of them involved shopping for shoes with her mom, unless those shoes were metal and made by a farrier. If there even was a farrier in the Millfields Shopping Center . . .

But by Saturday, Kizzy remembered, Mr. and Mrs. Kozlow would be back and Donut would be evicted. All the hay would be finished and a jar of honey certainly wouldn't buy any more. By Saturday, in fact, Kizzy would no longer have a pony at all.

Kizzy felt sick. She was exhausted, all out of dreams

and schemes. So she said, "Yes, Mom, that sounds great," and wondered how it was possible that the sight of her heart shattering into a million tiny pieces and scattering all over the plates of potatoes and beans did not keep anyone else from eating their dinner.

CHAPTER TWELVE

"Kizzy, why are there horse heads in the margins of your worksheet?" Mr. Wilson stood over Kizzy and tapped her table accusingly.

Because I still can't get the legs right was the answer Kizzy would have liked to give. "I'm sorry, Mr. Wilson. Doodling helps me concentrate."

"If that's the case, perhaps you could try doodling numbers and multiplication signs next time." He moved on to the next table. Mr. Wilson was mostly nice.

The bell rang for the end of the day. Everyone scraped their chairs back and started stuffing books into their backpacks.

"Finish that at home; everything you need is on the worksheet," shouted Mr. Wilson over the hubbub. "And don't forget to bring in your bottle rockets for our experiment on Friday!"

"Can you come with me and Donut?" Kizzy asked Pawel. "Hairnet or no hairnet, I'm going to master rising trot now, I just know it. Donut actually trotted in the park this morning. I think he remembered the dogs and wanted to get through it as quickly as he could. It was bouncy, though. My butt is sore and school chairs are hard."

"Don't talk to me about bruises. I'm purple all down one side from falling off your crazy bronco pony," said Pawel. "But yes, I'll come. GranPam's picking up the twins today."

At the former gas tank site, Kizzy was trying to mount, hopping around with one foot in the stirrup, when she and Pawel were surprised by Ali on her scooter. She skidded to a halt, breathless and panicked-looking. Donut's hay net was hanging over the scooter's handlebars. Ali threw it dramatically on the ground.

"Stop!"

"What are you doing out on your own? That's not allowed—you'll get us both into trouble," said Pawel.

"I know. I sneaked out. You'll thank me—I'm a hero. It's Mom and Dad."

"What about Mom and Dad?"

"They're back! You've got to come home and help me and Lopa clean up the shed before they notice it's a stable."

"What do you mean they're back? I thought they were supposed to be with Dziadek and Babcia until Friday?"

"That's the worst part: they're back with Dziadek and Babcia, who have decided Marek is so noisy that they need to come and stay and help. They've brought lots of treats with them, so that's good, but Dziadek keeps pinching my cheeks and Babcia is looking in all the closets and muttering things in Polish and making GranPam mad because she doesn't understand and Marek's screaming and screaming again and you've got to come!"

"OK, OK. Let's go." Pawel took Ali's hand. "Where

are they going to sleep? I'm not giving up my bed again."

"Hellooo!" said Kizzy. "What about Donut? Where's he supposed to go?"

Pawel turned around, smiled sadly, and shrugged. "I'm sorry, Kizz, but you knew this was going to happen. You'll have to turn him in now."

"BUT I HAD TWO MORE DAYS!" Kizzy shouted, startling Donut. "Two more days," she said again more quietly, soothing the pony with a pat.

"It was never guaranteed. I was running out of excuses to keep GranPam out of the yard anyway. Go back to city hall, Kizzy; they'll help," said Pawel. "See you, pal. It's been interesting," he added, patting Donut's neck.

"Goodbye, Donut. I'll never forget you." Ali hugged the pony tightly, then she and her brother both hurried off.

Alone, angry, and upset, Kizzy finally managed to mount Donut. She gathered up her reins and pushed Donut forward with new urgency. Donut, whether sensing the kind of businesslike attitude that P. A. Pickford would have approved of or just because he was finally in a cooperative mood, sprang into a reasonably paced trot.

Kizzy bounced around on top of him as they went around the makeshift ring. She felt no sense of accomplishment. Her fat tears dropped onto Donut's neck.

"What . . . can . . . I . . . do? What . . . can . . . I . . . do?"

The words thumped out of her with each jolting step. The rhythm set a beat; Kizzy started to rise and fall in the saddle in time with it. Suddenly it was easy! She could post the trot. She really could! Trotting was much more comfortable this way.

Her chant changed to "I . . . can . . . do . . . it! I . . . can . . . do . . . it!"

Kizzy wiped away her tears. She'd find another place for Donut. He wasn't leaving her yet, that was for sure — not now that they could trot.

* * *

Getting into Constable Towers was trickier this time. Kizzy and Donut arrived when most people were getting home from work. Finding a moment when the coast was clear enough to cross the lobby was difficult. Skulking in the shadows, Kizzy watched people come and go while Donut grazed. With horror, she saw first Jem and then her mom enter the building. Her emergency plan to put Donut back in her bedroom was going to be a whole lot harder now that both of them were already home.

At least there was no sign of Mr. Newman. Hopefully he was safely up on the roof with his bees. Kizzy could see a few of his workers buzzing in and out of the flowers growing in the concrete planters that flanked the entrance.

When there was finally a lull in foot traffic, Kizzy decided they'd better risk it. It took a lot of cajoling and a lot of pulling to get Donut away from the grass. As they passed the planters he stopped to snatch off the flowers, leaving them exposed.

"No, Donut! We can't stop here! If you eat any of Mr. Newman's bees by mistake, he'll never forgive me. Come on!"

After a very long minute, and only after every nasturtium had been decapitated, Donut relented. Kizzy led him into the lobby.

Donut entered the elevator like an old pro and Kizzy pressed the button for the twelfth floor. Her heart pounded as they went up; she had no idea how to manage the next part. If they were really, really quiet, and Mom was watching TV and Jem was in his room, could they sneak past? But her mom always wanted to see her when she heard her key turning in the lock. . . .

Kizzy tried to prepare a short and convincing speech. There was the logical approach: "So I got a new pet. He's going to be much easier to take care of than Nibbles was because he won't fit down the garbage disposal, so you're definitely not going to have to spend all night trying to tempt him out with a sunflower seed if he escapes. . . ."

Or perhaps something more dramatic: "Don't be mad, but I promised to take care of this pony for a while because his owner's in the hospital to have a terrible operation and otherwise the pony is going to be shot!"

Or she could play it cool and casual: "Yo, Momma. Meet Donut. He's going to hang with us. No problemo."

Or there was the truth: "I love him. I can't live without him."

She was thinking so hard about which approach to take that Kizzy didn't notice the elevator slowing until she looked up and saw they had only reached the eighth floor. Someone else had pressed the call button. She felt sick.

The elevator stopped and the doors began to open. Kizzy froze.

"Look, Mommy! A horsey!" They were faced with a very small boy, strapped in a stroller. He pointed a stubby finger at Donut and giggled. "A horsey! A horsey! Clippety-clop! Clippety-clop!" He rocked back and forth and tried to reach out to the pony.

Donut looked back at him, impassive. He was still chewing on a nasturtium.

"Quit wriggling, Benji. I can't find my purse."
The toddler's mother was crouched down and rummaging through the contents of the stroller's basket,
her face hidden.

"A horsey!" yelled the toddler.

"Going up or down?" asked Kizzy, still frozen.

"No, we need to go back and find it. You go on without us."

"A horsey!" screamed the toddler at full red-faced throttle as Kizzy jabbed and jabbed her finger on the twelfth-floor button and prayed.

The doors slowly slid shut. Kizzy caught a glimpse of the woman's startled face as she stood up and saw Donut through the narrowing gap before the doors closed completely and the elevator moved on up.

Kizzy and Donut got out at the twelfth floor and stood outside the door of the apartment. Kizzy's hand hovered with the key by the lock, then she put her ear to the door and listened instead. Donut swished his tail and nibbled on Kizzy's sleeve.

The TV was on and there were clanking sounds coming from the kitchen.

"What's cooking, Mom?" Jem's voice called.

"Donuts!" her mom replied, making Kizzy jump guiltily. Her faintest of faint hopes that her family might have gone back out or be locked in a convenient sound-proof box in the farthest corner of the apartment withered and died. She took a deep breath and looked to the ceiling for inspiration.

Kizzy put her key back in her pocket and led Donut away from the front door. This time they didn't go to the elevator. They went to the stairwell and began to climb.

CHAPTER THIRTEEN

"You've brought the feller to visit at last!"

Miss Turney beamed as she opened the door and greeted Kizzy and Donut like it was perfectly normal to find a pony on her doorstep.

"I know I shouldn't have, but I wasn't sure where else to go," said Kizzy. "I'm kind of stuck."

"Course you should have. You're always welcome. Stuck, you say?"

"Yes." Kizzy looked down at her feet, embarrassed. "You see, when I told you my mom knew all about Donut, that wasn't completely the truth."

"I expect it wasn't," said Miss Turney. "Good thing I can't remember exactly what you told me. Why don't you come in and tell me what's going on? You too, mister." Miss Turney stroked Donut's nose.

The three of them almost got stuck negotiating the hallway down to the kitchen. Kizzy had forgotten how cramped Miss Turney's apartment was. Donut's belly brushed against the walls as he stepped over the piles of papers and boxes.

Miss Turney was unconcerned. She opened the door to the balcony at the corner of the kitchen. The balconies at Constable Towers weren't large, but at least this was one space that was clutter-free.

"You'll fit nicely out there," Miss Turney said to Donut. "You can put your head through the door for your cookies."

Miss Turney was right: the balcony was the perfect size for a pony. Surrounded by a high concrete wall, it was quite safe, too. Donut could poke his nose over the top to sniff the air, but he certainly couldn't jump over even if he'd wanted to. And, Kizzy thought, there were no latches he could undo, either.

Miss Turney put the kettle on and made herself tea in an old brown teapot. She poured water for Donut into

a large bowl and added two sugar lumps, then dropped two cookies on top to make a kind of cookie-sludge soup. Kizzy thought it looked disgusting, but Donut's nostrils widened and he whickered enthusiastically.

"That's how Robbie used to like it. My dad would make it for him every day when they'd finished their rounds. Got to let it marinate a little first before you drink it, feller." Miss Turney kept the concoction out of Donut's reach and swirled it around. "Now then, why don't you start at the beginning?" she said to Kizzy.

Kizzy took a bite of her cookie and wondered where the beginning was. "I found Donut in the supermarket last Friday—the one on Heatherington Road. His real name's probably not Donut, but that's what I've been calling him."

"Suits him."

"Yes, I think it does. Anyway, I sort of reported him, and I've been sort of looking out for news about a lost horse, but maybe I haven't reported him as well as I should have because I was so happy to have him, and I think he's been happy to have me, too. I only wanted to keep him for a little while, and he was staying in my friend Pawel's shed, only now Pawel's mom and dad are back from Poland with baby Marek, who screams all the time, so Donut can't stay there anymore, and Pawel said I should turn him in but I don't want to. But I don't have anywhere else to put him and I can't keep him in my bedroom because Mom isn't ready for a pony in the apartment, although maybe she would be if I could make her understand, and I've only just learned to trot and maybe I could learn to canter, too, and I just love him *so* much and I don't know what to do."

Kizzy stopped and took a breath and another mouthful of cookie.

Miss Turney gave Donut's bowl another stir and then placed it on the counter by the door. They both watched as Donut sunk his muzzle in and slurped the brown soup enthusiastically. There was a lot of noise and splatter, and in a few seconds the bowl was empty. Donut nudged it back across the counter as if he were Oliver Twist asking for more. Miss Turney and Kizzy laughed and refilled his bowl with water.

"We all love our ponies," said Miss Turney. "Here, let me find my Robbie for you; won't take a minute."

She got up and disappeared into another room. Kizzy had a moment of panic that she was going to bring in a stuffed horse's head or a skeleton—it didn't seem impossible that her neighbor could have one hidden under all the boxes and bags. To her relief, Miss Turney came back a few minutes later with a battered brown photo album.

"There he is," she said, removing a photo from the album and holding it out to Kizzy.

Kizzy studied the picture. There was Miss Turney as a girl, standing proudly next to a pony harnessed to a wooden cart heaped with crates of fruit and vegetables. Miss Turney looked about ten; her hair hung down in two neat braids, and she was wearing a gingham dress and knee socks and smiling. The pony was perhaps a little bit taller than Donut, although certainly no fatter. The photo was in black and white, but it was still easy to see he shared Donut's chestnut coloring.

That was where the resemblance ended. This pony was curling up his lip and showing the whites of his eyes, as if he didn't want to be photographed. He looked like he might have bitten Miss Turney's braids right off just after the picture was taken. Donut was an angel who would never do such a thing. On the back of the photo someone had written "Dora and Robbie, 1949."

"Wasn't he a beauty? Feisty feller, though," said Miss Turney, gazing at the photo fondly.

"He looks it," said Kizzy. "Lucky you. Did you have him for a long time?"

"Ah, not as long as I'd have liked. My dad sold him when we had to leave the house with the yard. A man with a clipboard said all the houses in the street were going to come down. There were a lot of changes in those years, everything starting new after the war. So we got an apartment with a bathroom and Dad bought a van for work. He said it was better all around."

Miss Turney looked sad. "I cried for a week when Robbie left. I didn't understand why he couldn't come with us." She smiled up at Donut, who was chewing the edge of a towel. "And it turns out I was right, wasn't I? A pony fits in an apartment just fine."

Miss Turney and Kizzy grinned at each other in perfect understanding.

"So," Miss Turney continued, "why don't we let your feller stay with me for the time being? I'd like the company and he'll bring back memories."

"Oh, thank you so much!" said Kizzy. "I'll come and get him every morning and take him out. You'll barely know he's here, I promise."

"But I also think it's time you found out who he really belongs to, don't you? Your friend's not wrong about that. And that Mr. Newman doesn't miss much in this building—always after me to throw things away, the interfering old busybody. Sooner or later, dear, questions are going to be asked."

"I know," said Kizzy. "I'll do it as soon as I've cantered. Or maybe when I've jumped . . ."

One day at a time.

Kizzy rigged up Donut's hay net and filled up a bucket of water for him out on the balcony.

"I'll come first thing in the morning for him. Will that be OK?" she asked as she was leaving.

"That'll be fine, dear. Sleep doesn't come as easy these days and I'm always up with the pigeons," Miss Turney replied.

"Be good, Donut," Kizzy commanded finally. She left Donut and Miss Turney sharing stories about pony life in the city, one of them doing more talking than the other.

Downstairs, the tray of donuts Kizzy's mom had made was sitting out on the kitchen table. Kizzy filled her pockets with them for her, Miss Turney, and Donut to have for breakfast.

That night as she lay in bed, she could hear the usual thumps and strange sounds coming through the ceiling, but now, listening to them made her happy. Some of those thumps were being made by her pony, just a thin layer of concrete and plaster away. Kizzy wondered if she even heard a faint whinny as she rolled over in bed. All was well with the world.

CHAPTER FOURTEEN

All was not well between Kizzy and Pawel. The next day, Kizzy avoided him during attendance and morning classes and hurried off to lunch alone. As she wandered casually toward the wildlife garden, Kizzy was aware of Pawel's stern gaze following her, but she ignored him. She had not risked climbing over to see Donut since the pond incident, but she still liked to eat her lunch close to her pony and talk to him softly through the leafy cover. It was enough to be near him.

"You've still got him, haven't you?" Pawel's shadow fell over Kizzy as she unwrapped her cheese sandwich. "He's in there again."

"Shh," said Kizzy. "Someone might hear you. And since you evicted him it's no longer any concern of yours, is it? I've found a much better stable for him, where he'll be loved and appreciated when I can't be with him."

She turned away and bit into her sandwich, but Pawel flopped down on the grass beside her.

"This is all going to end badly," he said.

"I repeat: it is no longer any concern of yours," said Kizzy.

Pawel sighed. "You're not being very fair. I didn't have any choice. You have no idea what it's like at home. Babcia packed my lunch today." He opened a small Tupperware box and gazed gloomily at a mixture of pickled vegetables and gray-looking dumplings. Kizzy glanced at it and thawed a little.

"Want a sandwich? I made extra for Donut, but it's probably better for both of you if you eat it."

Pawel took one and they ate in silence. Grinding horse teeth could be heard from the other side of the fence; Donut was also having his lunch. But then, Donut's meals were more or less continuous.

"I've learned how to post the trot," said Kizzy finally. "I can't let him go yet."

"So where's he staying?"

"In the apartment above us with Dora—that's Miss Turney. She loves having him. She came out with me this morning. I hoped she might be able to help me learn how to canter, but turns out her pony was the opposite of Donut—it was stopping she had trouble with. Riding's definitely more complicated than P. A. Pickford makes out. It seems to depend a lot on the horse."

"Who'd have thought it?" said Pawel, and Kizzy

punched him on the shoulder. They were friends again. Getting Donut to trot as well as he had done the day before was not as easy as Kizzy had hoped. The pony tried to go back to his preferred plod as they circuited that afternoon. But Kizzy was determined and — as proof that her riding skills were improving — Donut began to cooperate. He picked up his pace just as a distant wailing announced the arrival of Pawel with all his siblings. Ali and Lopa ran forward applauding.

"Wow, you're going fast! And you can do the up and downy thing. You look like a real rider!" called Lopa.

"Donut, I thought I'd never see you in real life again!" said Ali.

Kizzy sat back down in the saddle and slowed Donut to a walk, then stopped in front of the girls. She patted his neck and dismounted. Pawel was a little farther behind, pushing his wailing baby brother in the stroller.

"Sorry, hope the noise doesn't frighten Donut. We can't stay long anyway; I'm supposed to be walking Marek around the block to see if he'll settle down. Then Dziadek's meeting us at the park to buy us ice cream."

"I scream, you scream, we all scream for ice cream," said Lopa. "But Marek just screams." She stroked Donut's broad nose and blew into his nostrils to say hello.

Pawel reached into the stroller and picked up his little brother carefully. The baby's face was scrunched and red, wet with furious tears. "Look, Marek! Meet your first pony. Say hello to Donut."

Pawel held the baby expertly against his chest and bobbed him up and down gently. The baby seemed soothed by this mini version of rising trot; his wailing subsided. He caught sight of the pony, stared, and reached out his tiny fingers to touch Donut's warm side. There was a pause, and then, at exactly the same moment, Donut lifted his tail and farted and Marek let out an enormous burp.

Pawel, Kizzy, and the twins all burst out laughing.

Whether it was because of the noise or the relief brought by the release of it, Marek first smiled and then gurgled and chuckled himself.

"Wow!" Pawel exclaimed. "Did you hear that? He's never done that before! I didn't think he could. You made Marek laugh, Donut—you made him happy!"

"Of course he did," said Kizzy, patting Donut proudly. "It's what I've always told you: ponies make everyone happy."

"Well, almost everyone . . ." Ali said, suddenly looking thoughtful. "Do you think we could get the two of them to do that again? It would be great for Donut's profile on YouTube if you filmed it. It would show that horrible dog lady, wouldn't it, Lopa?"

Kizzy laughed. "Donut doesn't have a profile on YouTube!"

Ali and Lopa exchanged glances. There was a silence—a silence that seemed laden with meaning.

"What is it?" asked Pawel.

"Don't be mad," said Lopa. "We were looking at pony clips on Mom's laptop last night to make us feel better, because we missed Donut."

"We didn't think we'd ever see him again. We were so happy to find him on there," added Ali.

"What are you talking about?" asked Kizzy, starting to worry.

"Donut's gone viral!" Lopa said excitedly. "He's had lots of hits! We think he could have his own channel and everything. We could make his mane curly again and do live pony makeovers and—"

"SHOW ME," Kizzy interrupted.

She held out her phone. Ali took it. Under Kizzy's fierce gaze she laboriously typed "pony hope green" into the search box. Donut nuzzled at Kizzy's shoulder.

"There you go." Ali turned the phone around.

Kizzy snatched it and stared at the small screen. Her heart was pounding. The clip was called "Savage Pony Attack in Hope Green Park." It already had more than ten thousand views.

It was the footage shot by the owner of the Chihuahuas: only a minute long, but that was more than enough. The dog was shown rolling around theatrically while the woman screamed, "He's been attacked! My baby!" and the pony's bolt across the grass was filmed until he was out of sight. Kizzy could also be seen, chasing after him in her school uniform. She scanned the comments underneath the video. They were mostly from dog lovers outraged at the "unprovoked" attack, sharing strong opinions about who should be allowed to use public parks.

"Ooh," said Pawel, who had been watching at Kizzy's side.

"How COULD she? This is completely one-sided and unfair. I'll tell them about the importance of keeping animals under control."

Kizzy began to type a spirited defense of Donut in the comments. She didn't get far before she lost her connection. The message "Your credit has expired. Purchase more data" appeared on the screen.

"Typical," said Kizzy, putting her phone away in disgust.

"Maybe just as well," said Pawel. "It's probably not a good idea to get involved."

"Anyway, it's OK," piped up Lopa. "That one's mean, but the comments on the others are much nicer."

"Others?" echoed Kizzy. Her head was swimming.

"There's one of you and him in the grocery store—and one from the merry-go-round in the park. Oh, and there's another where he's escaping from a trailer, just like he escaped from our shed."

"What?" asked Pawel. "What trailer?"

"Such a clever pony, aren't you, gorgeous?" said Ali, throwing her arms round Donut's neck. The clever pony slobbered on her sweater.

"OK, let's have a look on my phone," said Pawel in a businesslike way. He put Marek back in his stroller; the baby immediately started crying again. "Sorry, Marek, this is important. There might be clues to Donut's real owner."

"Actually, I've got to go," said Kizzy. "I don't have time for this now. Come on, Donut."

"Kizzy—wait!" said Pawel. It was hard to hear him over Marek's increasingly loud bellows.

"Sorry, Pawel. This is all really interesting, but places to go, people to see, jobs to do, you know how it is. Catch up tomorrow! See you, Ali! See you, Lopa! See you, Marek!"

Kizzy gave a cheery wave and walked Donut away

as briskly as he'd allow, then broke into a jog. There was a tight band around her chest and a boulder-sized lump in her throat.

That night—after Kizzy had sneaked Donut up to the thirteenth floor without incident; after she'd had some cookies and chatted brightly with Dora, brushed Donut, and fed and watered him and then fed him some more; after she'd washed down the staircase to remove the

evidence of Donut's badly timed waterfall of pee; after she'd eaten a plate of Mom's leftovers with special fried rice—Kizzy went into her room and shut the door. She pulled her phone out and switched it back on. It buzzed with a string of messages and missed calls from Pawel. Kizzy glanced at them, gazed up at the ceiling, swallowed hard, and breathed deeply. And then, back on her home Wi-Fi, she opened up YouTube again. There were three other clips from Ali's search called "Horse in Supermarket Sweep!," "Playground Pony," and "Super Crazy Horse Escape!!!!!!!" Kizzy watched the first two with a sad half smile, reliving the best minutes of her life.

Then she tapped the third clip. The grainy footage on this one had a date and time stamped in one corner; it was a week old and had come from a gas station security camera. A gas station that Kizzy, hugging her pillow while she watched, recognized.

A Land Rover pulling a large old-fashioned horse trailer drove up to a pump. A man got out and filled the car's tank, then disappeared out of shot toward the cashier. The moment he was gone, a brown nose poked through the gap at the back of the trailer. Teeth nibbled at the latches skillfully. Then the back door flipped open and a shaggy-maned chestnut face looked out. Donut trotted, surprisingly briskly, straight down the ramp and out of view. The clip ended with the man returning, looking surprised at the open trailer and checking inside before shrugging, latching it back up, and driving away.

Even in her misery, Kizzy couldn't help laughing at Donut's daring. The footage came from the gas station behind the Heatherington Road supermarket, no question. It looked as if the smell of fresh pastries had encouraged the pony to undo the latch, just as the smell of the vegetable patch had caused his escape from Pawel's shed. He was a pony who knew how to get what he wanted. Kizzy sighed in admiration.

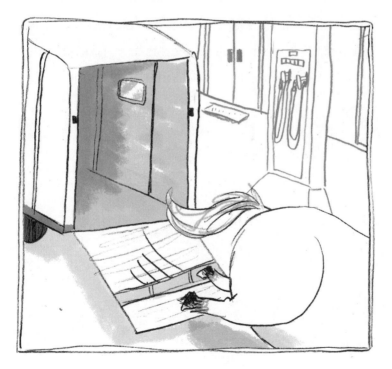

She watched the clip over and over. Why had the man just driven off without looking for him? She gazed at the blurry images of Donut, tears in her eyes. There was something else she couldn't ignore—something that was stamped in large letters around a logo of a rider in a helmet and jacket on the side of the trailer.

"Have u seen it yet? Look at side of trailer!!" one of Pawel's many texts had read.

The letters were fuzzy and out of focus, but Kizzy could just read them: PLUM ORCHARD RIDING STABLES — WHERE EXCELLENCE IS STANDARD.

That something else was Donut's real home.

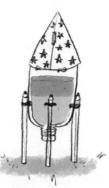

CHAPTER FIFTEEN

"So? SO?"

Pawel caught up with Kizzy in first period. The whole class had trooped onto the playground in a line. Under Mr. Wilson's excited supervision, they were going to launch rockets. While the teacher was distracted preparing a selection of homemade rocket fuels, including cola and mints, vinegar and baking soda, and a bucket of water with a bicycle pump, Pawel took the chance to interrogate Kizzy.

"Did you see it? What are you going to do? Did you call them?"

"I saw," said Kizzy. "And I don't know. I haven't called them, not yet." Her voice was flat. She felt flat.

She felt flat as a toothpaste tube from which every last bit had been squeezed out.

Pawel put his hand on Kizzy's arm gently. "I looked up the stables. They're very nice, aren't they? A good place for Donut, I think. Not a burger factory."

"Yes," agreed Kizzy hopelessly. "The stables seem nice."

In fact, Plum Orchard Riding Stables seemed more than nice. Kizzy had also looked up their website last night. They were just outside the city—no distance at all and yet a whole world away at the same time. The photos online showed everything Kizzy longed for: rows of gleaming stalls; girls and boys in real riding gear cantering around an indoor ring and hopping over red-and-white striped jumps; ribbons and trophies and a price list that started at forty dollars for a half-hour lesson. All in all, a much better place for a pony to live than a balcony on the thirteenth floor of Constable Towers.

Kizzy supposed she would call the stables after school and tell them to come and pick up Donut. Her one-day-at-a-time miracle had run out. There would be no cantering or jumping or figuring out how to draw horse legs. There would be no pony now. There would never be a pony ever again.

"I'm sorry, Kizzy. At least you got a week with Donut, huh?"

"That makes it worse," burst out Kizzy, suddenly unreasonably mad at Pawel. She didn't want to start crying at school. There had been enough of that into her pillow last night and into Donut's mane this morning. "I wish we'd never found him. I wish I didn't know how happy having a pony and riding every day made me feel."

Mr. Wilson looked up from his preparations. He had the wild gleam of enthusiasm teachers sometimes get when they've left their classroom. "Talking again, Kizzy and Pawel? No serious faces and discussions allowed until break time. This is going to be fun science! Kizzy, where's your bottle rocket? Get it ready for launch!"

Kizzy was pleased to have a distraction. She pressed a finger firmly in the corner of each eye to stop her tears and without thinking bent down and unzipped the main pocket of her backpack.

It was not the right compartment for her rocket. It was the compartment where Donut's manure—where Donut's manure from yesterday was still stored. Kizzy had forgotten to make her usual delivery to Pawel's neighbor yesterday after the shock of finding out about Donut's YouTube career. She tried to shut it again quickly but the zipper jammed.

"Phoooooooeeeeeeee! What's that smell? Mr. Wilson! Something stinks—something stinks really bad!"

Everyone near Kizzy held their noses and waved their hands in front of their faces.

"It's Kizzy's backpack that stinks! Ugh, Kizzy's bag is full of manure, Mr. Wilson!" said Jason Jones, pointing. Kizzy had never liked Jason Jones.

"I can explain—" began Kizzy, red-faced and tugging furiously at the zipper.

Mr. Wilson was too excited to listen. "Ready for our first launch? Five, four, three, two . . ."

Pawel nudged Kizzy sharply with his elbow. "Kizzy, look! Where are they going?"

A line of small children was snaking solemnly from the elementary side of the school. They were clutching wind chimes made from egg cartons and yogurt cups, on their way to hang them up, heading toward a leaf-covered fence.

"One!" Mr. Wilson dropped mints into a two-liter bottle of cola.

Jason Jones kicked Kizzy's backpack across the pavement, scattering its stinky contents.

Miss Okolo, the kindergarten teacher, opened the gate to the wildlife garden.

Whooooooooooooooooooooooooooooosh! A fountain of cola ten feet high shot frothing into the air.

"Poooo — Oooooooooooooooooooooooooooooh!" Kizzy and Pawel's classmates forgot to hold their noses and looked up, impressed.

"Aaaaaaaaaaaaaaaaaaaaaaaaaaaaaaah!" Thirty kindergartners and their teacher screamed in surprise and ran across the playground, dropping wind chimes, squelching balls of horse manure, and becoming drenched in a shower of cola.

Clip-clop, clip-clop, clip-clop, clip-clop. A shaggy brown shape pushed through the wildlife garden gate and trotted across the pavement. It came to a stop beside the fallen rocket and slurped up the minty remains lying in a fizzing puddle on the ground, swishing its tail happily.

"Guess he smelled those mints," said Pawel.

"Is that . . . Is that a horse?" asked Jason Jones, his eyes wide.

Kizzy stepped forward, skillfully dodging the scattered poop, and grabbed Donut's halter. "Hello, Donut," she said calmly. "Honestly, Jason, he's not a horse,

he's a pony." She pulled Donut's lead rope out of her pocket and clipped it to his halter.

All around her there was uproar. Windows were thrown open and heads were poking out to see what all the screaming was about. The classes on the ground floor were already streaming out onto the playground.

"There's a pony on the playground!"

"A pony on the playground?"

"A pony! On the playground!"

A growing crowd clustered around Kizzy and Donut. Kizzy knew she should have felt despair. The worst was finally happening. The consequences were going to be disastrous. Her life was over.

Surprisingly, she found she felt much more cheerful. Her life had been over anyway. If these were going to be her last hours of pony ownership, she would rather be spending them with Donut—whatever the consequences.

The first consequence arrived in the form of Ms. Khan, the principal, all pointy shoes and big hair and shiny buttons. The crowd hushed respectfully at the sound of her step.

"What is the meaning of this? Where has this animal come from?" she asked, then shrieked, "Ugh!" as one heel sank into some manure.

Holding Donut's rope, Kizzy stepped forward bravely. "He's mine. Sort of. I've been keeping him in the wildlife garden, where he's been trimming the grass and eating the rubbish. I'm sorry, but there was nowhere else to keep him. I'll take him home now."

"Immediate suspension! I'm calling your mother, Kezia. I'm very disappointed in you. And somebody get this animal off school property. Somebody get this animal off me!"

Unfortunately, Donut was showing an interest in Ms. Khan's jacket. Kizzy assumed he'd gotten a whiff of some hidden treat in one of the pockets. What did principals keep in their pockets to get them through the day? She guessed it wouldn't be sensible to let Donut find out.

Kizzy pulled Donut away from temptation, collected her backpack, put on her bike helmet, and marched straight out of the school gates. She didn't look back. From somewhere behind her Ali and Lopa called, "Goodbye, Donut! Goodbye for real this time!" And then she was around the corner and out of earshot.

"Look at us! We showed the whole school," Kizzy said to Donut. "There's nothing we can't do together. The world is ours now."

She led her pony down the street with an enormous

grin on her face, no longer caring how many people saw them or what they thought. Mr. Wilson's face! Jason Jones's face! Ms. Khan's face! Kizzy started to giggle. Then she started to laugh. And then she started a kind of hiccuping, whooping braying that was less fun but that she didn't seem to be able to stop.

Donut waited with his eyes half-closed, enjoying the sun on his back. He ignored both the passing traffic and the hysterical girl on the other end of his lead rope.

After a few minutes, Kizzy began to calm down and stop hiccuping. She leaned into Donut's solid, warm side and tried to figure out what to do next. He leaned back into her, and for once he didn't nibble or bite or look for food. They stayed like that for several breaths, until Kizzy felt steady and sure once again.

"OK, Donut, or whatever your name really is, I am going to take you home myself. To your real home, that is," said Kizzy. "I want to see you happy there, with all those real riders. That'll make me not being a real rider easier, I think."

Donut snorted, which Kizzy took for approval and deep sympathy.

"But before we go, there's someone I'd like you to meet." Kizzy started to lead Donut down a road she'd always been very careful to avoid until now.

The Sunshine Café was living up to its name. Its red-and-yellow awning was pulled out and a few tables were on the sidewalk. Kizzy saw her mom before her mom saw her. She was bringing out sandwiches and fries and plates of sausages to a table of construction workers in fluorescent jackets.

"Mom!" Kizzy called.

Her mom turned at Kizzy's voice. She put her hand up to shade her eyes and blinked. Then she put her hand down to steady herself on one of the tables. "Kizzy?"

Kizzy prepared to deliver her best explaining speech. She imagined a dignified moment of forgiveness, her mother stroking Donut and saying she understood and would clear everything with Ms. Khan before she suspended Kizzy.

But Donut had other ideas. The smell of fries and toast and pastries was wafting down the street in the warm breeze. He seemed to know that the fries at the Sunshine Café were particularly good: thick and crunchy and golden, with soft fluffy middles.

"Oh, sorry, Mom! Whoa, Donut!" said Kizzy. She tried to dig her heels into the ground, but the sidewalk offered no resistance. Her pony put his head down in determination and pulled Kizzy forward, jolting her arms half out of their sockets.

"Kizzy? Who gave . . . ? What have . . . ? Where did . . . ?" Kizzy's mom struggled to find words. Donut wasn't interested in listening to them anyway. He barged through the tables, knocking chairs over, and stuck his nose straight into one of the construction workers' plates of food. He snatched half a plateful with one sweep of his tongue.

"Hey! Nobody steals my fries!" The construction worker squared up to Donut as his friends laughed. He drew his arm back, his fingers curling into a fist.

Kizzy made another of her quick decisions. Using one of the café chairs as an emergency mounting block, she scrambled onto Donut's bare back.

"Sorry, Mom," she said. "Lots to say — mainly sorry — but turns out now's not the time. Come on, Donut!"

She squeezed his sides harder than she'd ever done before. Whether because he didn't like the look of the construction worker's fist, or because of her confident aids, or simply because he wanted to, Donut responded immediately. Finally, pony and rider were in perfect harmony as Donut scooted away. And, with Kizzy clinging on and whooping, Donut cantered — actually cantered — down the street.

"KIZZY!" yelled her mom as they disappeared.

CHAPTER SIXTEEN

Donut's mane streamed upward into Kizzy's face. She grabbed a hunk of it and gripped it tightly, crouching low, trying to keep her balance. Her backpack thumped against her back. Without a saddle or a bridle, this was one ride that Donut was going to stay firmly in charge of, but Kizzy didn't care. The speed made her feel powerful, almost invincible. Donut's long-awaited canter was beautifully smooth and fluid.

As they raced along, the sidewalks, buildings, and surprised people passed in a glorious blur. A cyclist swerved out of the way to avoid them, and a mailman abandoned his cart and jumped over a low shrub. The rush of wind made Kizzy's eyes sparkle and her cheeks tingle, and she started to laugh. This was riding. This was wonderful. She felt bigger, more herself, more alive. It was everything Kizzy had ever dreamed of.

And then, far too quickly, it was over. They careered around a corner and up onto some grass. Donut skidded to an abrupt halt, put his head down, and started grazing. Now Kizzy did lose her balance; she slid all the way down Donut's neck, right over his ears, and made bumpy contact with the grass. With a soppy smile still plastered on her face, she rolled onto her back and squinted up. Past Donut's munching silhouette she saw a high-rise building. They were right outside Constable Towers: home.

"You're not supposed to canter on roads, Donut. It's not good for your legs. We won't do it again—but I'm so glad you did it just this one time." Kizzy sighed with contentment.

The sun disappeared behind a cloud. Then Kizzy blinked; it wasn't a cloud that was casting a shadow. It was a silhouette.

"What is that doing on MY grass?" the silhouette said.

Kizzy's contented smile dissolved. She scrambled up and brushed herself down. "Ah," she began. "Hello, Mr. Newman. Yes . . . I was going to introduce you, but I've been waiting for the right moment. This is Donut—"

"Hoofprints on the grass—I thought I was going mad. Whinnying in the middle of the night, said Mr. Feisal in 13D—I told him he was going crazy. A very large animal in the elevator, said Mrs. Blake in 8C. A lingering smell that had me lifting manhole covers and getting the drains checked. And all along it was you! Thought you'd make a fool of an old man, did you? Thought you'd try to sneak behind my back?"

"No!" said Kizzy. "It all happened by accident. I found this pony and I thought it would be OK if he stayed here for a little while, that's all."

"Well, it's not OK. Not OK at all. And I can tell you what's going to happen right now: I'm calling the animal control officer to remove this thing. And then I'll be calling the housing association so they'll give your family notice to leave my building—that's what's going to happen."

All the joy Kizzy felt at having cantered disappeared. She felt sick. Being suspended from school was one thing, but this . . .

"No! Please no! You can't do that. It's not Mom and Jem's fault—they never even knew. Please, Mr. Newman!"

"Should have thought before you broke the rules. They're quite clear. Everybody signs them on their

rental agreement: 'Animals only with written permission, and no dangerous animals.' To think I saw you as one of the good ones. You were lying to me all the time, taking advantage of my good nature."

"I wasn't, honest! I liked helping you. I'll help you more and I'm taking Donut away now, back to his real home. Please don't report me!" Kizzy pleaded, but Mr. Newman was too furious to listen.

"Harry!" There was a shout from the doorway of the building. "Stop bullying that good girl!"

Mr. Newman turned around. Miss Turney was marching up to them. She looked fiery in a way Kizzy hadn't seen before—feisty, even.

"Now, Dora," said Mr. Newman, "this is no concern of yours. Don't get me started. Your junk is bad enough. I turn a blind eye because you've been here so long but—"

"Been here a sight longer than you, haven't I? I've seen plenty of people come and go—animals and caretakers, too, in fact. And I don't see how these two have been any trouble at all," said Miss Turney, standing firm in her slippered feet.

"You can't keep livestock in a high-rise apartment building. It isn't right. The rules are there for a reason. It could have caused any number of incidents. That animal is a danger and a liability."

Mr. Newman pointed a finger accusingly at Donut. The danger and the liability did not stop grazing.

"That's nonsense. He was wonderful company when he stayed with me," said Miss Turney. "Helped me sort through boxes and remember what I was doing. I have trouble remembering when I'm on my own."

"You were in on it, too? I might have known. You've gone too far this time, Dora. I'm sorry but I'm going to have to let Social Services know. It's time you were moving into a more suitable accommodation for someone your age. You need someone to keep an eye on you."

"Don't say that!" said Kizzy. "Miss Turney's fine just where she is!"

But Miss Turney didn't need her help. She wasn't finished yet. "Sounds like you've got a lot of phone calls to make, Harry. You better get started right away. Only, I wonder if you might want to get your bees first? If the ones I saw swarming by the Whistler apartments this morning are your bees. I was thinking they might be a danger to the public—one that the city or the housing association or Social Services would be interested in hearing about. You have written permission for them?" she said slowly.

Kizzy's spirits lifted.

"My bees are swarming? Why didn't you say so earlier? I have to get them before some neighborhood hooligan upsets them. Easily disturbed in the wrong hands are bees." Mr. Newman's red face of fury blanched pale with worry, and he hurried away.

"Don't mind that one." Miss Turney turned to Kizzy. She smiled and patted Donut. "There's a lot of bluster, but he's got a good heart. He'll come around. You taking this one back now, dear?"

Kizzy nodded miserably.

"Ah, well, it's time, I suppose. It was nice to have a reminder of the old days. Used to be plenty of horses and ponies around here." Miss Turney sighed and produced yet another package of cookies from her coat pocket. She handed them to Kizzy. "Take these for the trip, and come and tell me all about it when you're done. My door's always open for a cookie."

"I will. You can be sure of it," said Kizzy, giving the old lady a hug. "I'm sorry I never came before. Thank you for everything."

"Goodbye, feller," said Miss Turney to Donut. "Lovely boy. Hope to see you again one of these days." She ran her hand down his nose and Donut bowed his head.

"Come on, Donut. We've got a ways to go," said Kizzy, putting the cookies into the section of her backpack that didn't stink of poop. Donut had shaved all available grass down to a buzz cut. He was happy to follow.

Kizzy had calculated it was about twelve miles in a straight line to the stables—a long walk, but manageable on a pleasant, sunny day. The problem was the straight line part. What with all the streets and houses and traffic, going straight all the way to the stables was impossible. Kizzy tried to find patches of free Wi-Fi to plot a route on her phone, but her battery was running low.

"Perhaps we could find our way using the sun and stars?" she suggested to Donut as they walked. "Or do you know your way home, like a sniffer dog or a pigeon?"

In Kizzy's books, lost ponies could find their way across plains in terrible blizzards. Navigating on a sunny day didn't seem too much to ask. She tried letting Donut lead the way, but he just stopped at the nearest available edible greenery. Their progress was slow.

"Wait a minute. Look, Donut! If we get to the river, we can follow it to the stable. I think it passes right by Plum Orchard Stables," Kizzy said, squinting at her phone. The screen went black, out of battery as well as signal now. Kizzy put it back in her pocket. She knew the river anyway: it was the brown ribbon that snaked past the Millfields Shopping Center. She and her mom sometimes took the bus out there if they needed something from a big store. How to get there now?

Fifteen minutes later, Kizzy climbed on board the number 301 bus and casually pressed her bus pass on the driver's machine.

"Just one moment, please. I'm bringing my, um,

assistance animal on board," she said in as businesslike a way as possible. She popped out and loaded Donut through the back doors. It was lucky there were no strollers and the wheelchair space was empty. The pony just fit in; his butt stuck out all the way to the double doors, but there was room to close them without his tail getting caught. Kizzy held Donut's head and smiled politely at the other passengers. They stared back.

The driver rapped sharply on his window, then swung the flap open and stuck his head out.

"What do you think you're doing? You can't bring a pony on a bus!"

"Are you sure?" asked Kizzy.

"Of course I'm sure!"

"No, really," said Kizzy in her most reasonable voice. "Has anyone ever said to you in your training that ponies aren't allowed on buses?"

"It's common sense!"

"But not a rule," said Kizzy. "You let dogs on all the time, and Donut's not that much bigger."

"But anything could happen!"

"Does he look like trouble? I bet you get much worse on the night buses after the bars close."

"Ah, you're trying to confuse me now," said the driver. He looked at Donut uncertainly. The pony was standing very peacefully, with one hoof resting up and his eyes half-closed.

"Come on, driver." An old lady spoke up. "The coffee and a muffin for a dollar deal will be over before I get there if we don't leave soon. Drive!"

CHAPTER SEVENTEEN

The bus trip went smoothly. Donut tried to nibble the seats, but Kizzy managed to distract him with one of Miss Turney's cookies, and a toddler gave him a handful of squashed blueberries, too. He was certainly a conversation starter. Normally, in Kizzy's experience, people on buses did everything they could to avoid talking or meeting anyone else's eye. Having a pony on board changed that. Kizzy had to answer a lot of questions: "What's his name?" "Where did you get him?" "Does he bite?" They were also filmed by several people on their phones. Donut's YouTube profile looked likely to grow—he really would be able to have his own channel soon.

At the shopping center everyone piled off the bus as friends. Not even the discovery of a muddy hoofprint on a lady's shopping bag dampened spirits. Donut got lots of pats. He stood and basked in the admiration.

"Thank you, driver!" called Kizzy with a wave. The driver scurried off to the break room without waving back. He looked like he needed a strong cup of coffee.

Kizzy and Donut skirted around the edge of the parking lot and found the path to the river. They squeezed through the metal gates and were soon walking along the path, past warehouses, storage depots, and scrubland. A few cyclists and walkers shot them curious looks as they passed, and there was an awkward moment when Donut pooped right in front of a man walking his dog. The man handed Kizzy a bag and then stood over her while she dealt with it. The bag was barely large enough, and Kizzy ended up having to pick up each ball separately.

After a while the industrial units petered out and they began to pass big houses instead. Some had yards that backed right up to the path; Donut stole mouthfuls of flowers from over their fences. The river looked more inviting here. There were ducks swimming, patches of reeds, and fewer abandoned shopping carts.

"We're not in Hope Green anymore, that's for sure." Kizzy looked at Donut. "Getting closer to your home?" she asked him.

Farther up, even the houses came to an end. Kizzy and Donut walked and walked. They passed under a concrete bridge, traffic thundering over their heads. On the other side they found themselves among fields and woods. The path widened. Now any walkers they met smiled at Kizzy and Donut or ignored them. They no longer stared as if the pony was out of place.

"Definitely closer to your home." Kizzy sighed. She couldn't bear to reach their destination quite yet. "Let's stop for a while."

She sat down under a tree. The sun was really hot now. Kizzy got the cookies and her squashed lunch out of her backpack, and she and Donut finished them together. As her pony grazed, Kizzy tried to drink in every tiny bit of him. He looked so beautiful with his mane hanging down over his eyes. The dappled sunlight shining through the leaves picked out the reddish-gold highlights of his coat. He sparkled as if still dusted with Ali and Lopa's glitter.

Kizzy rooted through her backpack once more. She pulled out a notebook and pencil. On page after page, as

the afternoon shadows lengthened, Kizzy drew Donut. She drew his head and his back and his stomach, and his legs and hooves. She drew each of his legs about five times, in fact, until she was satisfied she understood them.

"I've got it: they have to go a little in the wrong direction at the bottom before you make them go in the right direction! I understand now," she told Donut. He kept on eating, not very interested in his own legs.

Kizzy flopped back on the grass and gazed at him, trying to imprint in her memory every second that they were together. Her heart was full.

But time was almost up. Kizzy felt uneasy, aware of both her dead phone and the fact that, although she'd thought about the trip to Plum Orchard with Donut, she had not thought at all about the trip back without him. She'd have to do the same walk again with nothing to look forward to but the scolding-to-end-all-scoldings waiting at home. It would be best to do as much as she could before it got dark.

There could be one last ride before the start of a gray, hopeless, pony-less future. Kizzy tied the other end of the lead rope to Donut's halter to fashion reins and, with the help of a handy tree root, slid onto his warm back. Turning his head toward the path, Kizzy nudged Donut forward and they walked on. In the distance she could see buildings and a church spire. Remembering the map, Kizzy was pretty sure these marked both the end of the path — and an ending for her.

She remembered her first bareback ride on Donut. Could it really have been less than a week ago? He'd felt so high and wide then, and Kizzy had been so nervous. Now it felt as natural as walking on her own legs. The steady rhythm of the pony's amble was comforting and easy, although Donut still felt quite wide.

They walked under another bridge. The houses and church spire were very close now. Again Kizzy felt an urge to dawdle, to make the day last longer. Perhaps, even now, she didn't really have to take Donut back.

Look! Wasn't that a farmhouse over there? Suppose she knocked on the door and found a rosy-cheeked farmer? Suppose that farmer needed help bringing in the harvest? (Was it harvesttime? Surely there must be something to harvest.) Suppose the farmer gave them glasses of creamy milk and apples and freshly baked bread and suggested that Kizzy and Mom and Jem and Donut move rent free into his empty farm cottage with roses growing over the door and a paddock? Then Kizzy wouldn't have to go back to school and Mom wouldn't have to work at the café anymore. They could open up a restaurant selling pie and pictures of Donut that Kizzy would paint now that she knew how to draw the legs.

But Donut's ears were flicking back and forward as though he was starting to recognize his surroundings.

He was done dawdling. He picked up his pace and began to trot. Kizzy's daydreams were jolted rudely away as she slipped around on the pony's bumping back.

"Do you know the way from here?" asked Kizzy, torn between admiration for Donut's obvious intelligence and heartbreak at his eagerness to be home. She let him take complete charge of their direction. At the next fork, Donut swung off to the left, and the two of them went clattering up a muddy lane marked by a bridle path sign. Now there were other hoofprints visible on the track.

Donut veered right onto the grassy side of a road. Cars sped past much faster than city traffic. Kizzy felt a little nervous.

"Hang on, Donut. Whoa! Let me get off and lead you." But with no bridle to control him, Kizzy now found it as difficult to make Donut stop moving as she had once found making him start. All she could do was try to pull his nose away from the danger of the road. Which meant, as it turned out, pulling his nose in the direction of the exceedingly muddy ditch on the other side.

Donut didn't care. He scrambled down into the ooze, where the combination of the sticky ground and the edible temptations of the bushes on the other bank finally made him stop.

Kizzy took the opportunity to slip safely off his back. She landed squelching into the thick mud, which immediately claimed one of her shoes. Kizzy fished it out with two fingers and hopped back onto the grass. She wrung out her sock and wiped her shoe on the turf.

Having gotten the worst of the ditch off herself, Kizzy tugged on Donut's rope to encourage him out of it. The pony's hooves made a sound like a spoon scooping jelly as they were pulled out. When he clambered back up to the grass, Donut shuddered and shook his whole body like a wet dog, splattering Kizzy with flecks of dirt. Donut was now wearing four chocolate-brown mud stockings.

"Honestly, Donut! I was hoping to make a dignified entrance to your stables. Your real owner will never

believe I've been taking good care of you if they see us looking like this," said Kizzy. She gathered handfuls of long grass and rubbed the worst of the caked-on mud off the pony. Donut snatched and pulled at the handfuls as she worked.

Kizzy gave in and straightened up. And then she

saw the sign—not even twenty feet up the road. A sign reading PLUM ORCHARD with the same logo she had seen on the trailer in the YouTube video. Time was completely and absolutely up.

Kizzy swallowed. She turned and buried her head against Donut's neck one last time for a private goodbye.

"This is it, then—this is where you belong. They'd better love you like I love you," she whispered into the smooth expanse of chestnut hair and muscle.

But Donut was already tugging forward, impatient to be moving again. Kizzy, her heart breaking, led, or rather followed, him into the yard.

CHAPTER EIGHTEEN

In front of them was a scene of horsey industry. Heads poked out of rows of stalls: grays, chestnuts, bays, and even a palomino. Kizzy had never seen so many horses in one place. One or two adults and many more teenagers and children were moving between the stalls. Some of them had bridles hanging over their arms, on their way to tack up for a lesson, and others were holding brushes and buckets. One large shiny bay horse, with bright red polos on its legs, was being led out to a mounting block by a woman in a dark blue jacket and—Kizzy made a mental note to tell Pawel later—a hairnet under her helmet.

It was the kind of place where Kizzy had always dreamed of belonging; now that she was here she felt overwhelmed. She hovered near the entrance, hoping to watch for a while, but Donut had no patience for self-consciousness. He tugged her toward an open shed he seemed very familiar with. Containers of grain were visible inside. He lunged forward and stuck his head in for a snatch-and-grab raid.

"Aw, it's Pumpkin! Back to his old tricks, too." A girl about Kizzy's age put down the wheelbarrow she'd been pushing and pointed at Donut.

Kizzy looked around, confused for a moment, before realizing that Pumpkin was Donut. Pumpkin! What a ridiculous name. Just because he was sort of round and sort of orange. Donut suited him much better.

"Better not let Miss Pickford see him do that. Get out of there, Pumpkin!" An older girl with long blond hair and a competent, in-charge air came over and hauled Pumpkin-Donut's nose out of the feed bin. She shut the door to the shed firmly and smiled at Kizzy. "What's he doing back here anyway?"

Kizzy felt out of her depth. All her words and

explanations were lost. She could only stand and gawk uselessly at all these perfect pony people doing perfect pony things. To her embarrassment she started to cry.

"I found him. I've been taking care of him, but I thought I should bring him back now," she said, gulping away her tears.

"Oh, that was nice of you. But he doesn't—" The girl was interrupted by a furious volley of yapping. Two miniature terriers bounded over and began weaving in and out of Donut's legs, snapping and growling. The pony's ears immediately flattened and his back hunched in unhappiness. They weren't Chihuahuas in clothes but they were similar. Kizzy could tell that Donut knew this particular pair well—they had history.

"Pinky and Perky, come here! HEEL!" a commanding voice bellowed.

Kizzy turned around and saw a woman coming out of a small house on the other side of the property. She strode toward them, thwacking a riding crop against her boot. She was dressed in tweed and—another one for Pawel!—her hair was scraped into a net. Her age was difficult to guess. She was leathery skinned and as pinched as a prune. Kizzy had a feeling she'd seen her somewhere before.

"Uh-oh," muttered the blond-haired girl under her breath. "Now we're in for it."

The stable was emptying rapidly as the woman made her way toward them. Riders and helpers were trying to make themselves invisible by disappearing into stalls and doorways. The two dogs bounded back at the woman's call and trotted at her ankle, looking up with devotion.

Pumpkin-Donut also noticed the woman's approach. His nostrils flared in recognition, his ears went back, and he let out a sharp whinny. It appeared Kizzy had finally found his owner. How both of them felt about the reunion was yet to be seen.

The woman stared at Donut. "No, no, no!" she spluttered. "I was perfectly clear. Which idiot brought him back? This was a sale with no return — I will not have that animal causing chaos in my stables again."

Kizzy stopped feeling tearful. She felt angry. "I don't know what you're talking about, but I guess I'm that idiot. I rescued Donut — I mean Pumpkin. Sort of

rescued him. I love him anyway and I didn't want to return him, but when I saw the video of him escaping, I thought you must be missing him. *I* will miss him a lot. I thought this was a better place for him and that I was doing the right thing."

"Escape . . . video?" whispered the blond girl beside Kizzy. Kizzy glanced across at her.

"From the trailer. At the gas station—it's on YouTube."

She began to explain but the prune-faced woman wasn't listening to them. She was focused on Donut. She pointed an accusing finger at the pony.

"That animal"—the woman's voice was icy—"brings nothing but havoc. This is an establishment of excellence, where controlled horsemanship is achieved through discipline and rigor. There is no place here for lazy animals who escape from their stalls, eat their way through grain bins, the hay barn, and the hanging baskets, and then—the final straw—push their way into my house and eat THE CONTENTS OF MY FRIDGE!"

The woman's face had got redder and redder. She was now shouting directly at Pumpkin-Donut. He answered her by opening his mouth to show off the remains of the pilfered grain and then chomping back down on them.

Kizzy grinned: the lady's stories sounded familiar.

"I don't have much experience, but he does seem to be an unusually hungry pony. It's probably a growth spurt; that's what my mom says when my brother does the same thing," she said. She felt a great balloon of hope and happiness swelling inside. If she had come all this way only to discover that Donut was unwanted and in need of rehoming — if that was really true — then it didn't matter what Mr. Newman or Mom thought, Donut would be coming back to live with her and Miss Turney forever. But . . .

"I sold him with a bunch of others a week or two ago. It's not my problem if your new establishment can't handle him; I will not have this one back and there will be no refunds."

Kizzy's balloon deflated a little. "New establishment?"

"And," the woman continued, "if you are representative of the kind of rider they attract, I can see that dreadful pony has been well matched. You're both completely filthy! What sort of helmet do you call that? Where are your jodhpurs and boots? You would certainly not be allowed to ride in one of my lessons like that!"

Kizzy looked down at herself. Not only was her bottom half mostly mud, but her top half was covered in horsehair and grass stains and there was a large patch of slobber on her sweater where Donut had tried to grab a piece of cheese when it fell out of her sandwich.

She drew herself up. "I'm very sorry. I can see I've made quite a mistake coming here. Do—Pumpkin and I will not be bothering you anymore. We'll go back to our 'establishment,' which suits us much better anyway."

She nodded to the competent blond-haired girl, who was standing frozen. Kizzy tightened her grasp on the lead rope and marched back out of the yard. Donut came willingly, apparently satisfied with his raid on the grain bins. The dogs started yapping again as they left. Donut flicked up his back heels at them.

Just before she reached the road, Kizzy had a revelation. She turned round. "Oh!" she said. "Are you Miss Pickford? The same as P. A. Pickford, the author of *Correct Horsemanship for the Young Rider*?"

"I am." The prune-faced woman inclined her head.

"Ah," said Kizzy. "That explains a lot."

They turned back down the road. Kizzy patted Donut's neck. She couldn't think of him as Pumpkin quite yet. "But I'll give it a try if you prefer it," she promised him.

Kizzy was trying to feel victorious: they were still together, and Miss Pickford had practically said he was hers to keep. But what about this "new establishment" that had bought him?

Kizzy suddenly felt exhausted. She thought about Mom and Jem and Pawel and Mr. Newman and Miss Turney and everything waiting for her back home. How could she show up again with a pony when it might mean her family lost their home? And, having seen where he'd come from, it was clear Pumpkin-Donut did need a real stable—one with a door he could look over and bedding and other horses to keep him company.

A garden shed or a thirteenth-floor balcony was never going to be enough. Kizzy sighed. Everything had become too complicated.

It would be getting dark soon. Some cars were already putting their headlights on. Donut was trudging slowly. When they reached the turnoff to the bridle path he stopped walking altogether. He didn't pull or try to turn back to the stables, but Donut made it perfectly clear he was done for the day.

"Come on! We've barely begun—there are still twelve miles to walk," Kizzy tried to encourage him.

The pony showed no interest in Kizzy's pleading. He turned away, drooped his head, tipped his back foot up, and half closed his eyes.

"You can't go to sleep here by the road!" Kizzy said. But she knew she sounded half-hearted; she was worn out, too. Kizzy flopped down onto the grass. "We'll just rest for a little while then," she said. Tears started dripping down her face. She tried to wipe them away with her sleeve, but more and more kept falling.

Within a few minutes the tears had turned into all-out sobbing: the scrunched-up and puffy red-faced sort,

with added choking noises and bubbling snot. Even Donut noticed; he gently nudged Kizzy's shoulder. It only made her cry harder.

Kizzy was so caught up in her misery that Kizzy didn't notice the slowing headlights at first. A vehicle pulled up in the shoulder ahead and two figures got out. Donut stiffened, his ears pricked forward, and he snorted. Kizzy looked up, scared as well as miserable as she watched them approach.

They came closer. One of them was wearing jodhpurs and had long blond hair and a confident air. But the man with her looked familiar, too.

"Hello! We hoped we'd catch up to you. We've brought the trailer," the man said. "We wondered if you might like a ride?"

It was the man from the gas station video—the driver with the trailer.

CHAPTER NINETEEN

"Turns out Ned can't count to four. I should have known!" The blond girl from Plum Orchard, who had introduced herself as Carolyn, stuck her tongue out at her boyfriend sitting in the driver's seat of the Land Rover. Kizzy sat behind them on an old tartan blanket that smelled deliciously of dog and horse. She felt sad but relaxed. Nobody needed to walk any farther; Donut was safe, and so was she.

"That's not fair. Turns out you aren't very good at passing on instructions, or doing up latches on trailers. I had no idea how many were supposed to be back there. I was only the delivery driver," said Ned, sticking his tongue out back at her.

"I told you four!"

"You didn't! And they never said any were missing when I unloaded the others. How was I to know?"

"Miss Pickford was yelling while I was loading them in. I may have gotten distracted. But Pumpkin should be renamed Houdini; he's so clever with his teeth. He must have stood on something to reach the latch!"

"Miss Pickford is always yelling. I was hiding in the car from her horrible rat dogs. One of them took a chunk out of my finger last month." Ned glanced at his hand ruefully.

"Anyway." Carolyn smiled at Kizzy. "No harm done. Thanks for the tip-off about YouTube, Kizzy, and thank goodness Miss Pickford was too angry to pick up on that. Not that I expect she's ever even heard of YouTube. I hid in the tack room and looked up the whole thing after you left, then called Ned to fetch the trailer and come and find you. I'd no idea that he hadn't delivered all the horses last week. We both owe you our jobs. Even if Miss Pickford's not the easiest boss, I couldn't not work with horses."

They'd put a blanket on Donut, loaded him into the

trailer, and made him comfortable with some not-meant-for-a-rabbit hay. There had been explanations from Kizzy about her pony hiding and YouTube detective work. Now they all needed to decide what to do next.

"Sounds like you did a great job with Pumpkin, Kizzy. He's got a mind of his own that pony; that's why Miss Pickford put him up for sale. But it's a little late to deliver him to his new home," said Carolyn. "I'll turn him out in the field next to my place overnight, and we can take him first thing, can't we, Ned? I'm on a late shift at Plum Orchard tomorrow. We need to deliver you first though, Kizzy. Your family must be frantic."

Kizzy was trying to take everything in. She couldn't believe she was in a car pulling an actual, real trailer. There were tattered ribbons pinned up above the windshield and hair-covered dandy brushes lying on the dashboard. She'd thought she'd feel nervous and tongue-tied and out of place, but she felt surprisingly comfortable. Carolyn and Ned had been so nice. It was all ordinary to them, of course; it made her feel like it could be ordinary for her, too, one day.

"Can I borrow your phone to let my mom know

I'm OK?" Kizzy paused, then risked another question. "Where is Pumpkin's new home?"

"It's called Under Arches Farm," said Carolyn. "I know Miss Pickford agreed to sell them a few ponies, but I think there were arguments and they've been busy getting ready. I guess they got confused about which horses to expect when."

"A farm? You're sure they're going to really take

care of Pumpkin? They're . . ." Kizzy hesitated, "not going to eat him?"

Carolyn laughed. "Definitely not! I'm sure he'll be happy there. I'll leave a message telling them to expect us in the morning. Perhaps you'd like to come, too, help settle him in and explain to his new owners why he's a week late? If your mom will let you after today's adventures."

"Could I? That would be wonderful."

One more day with Donut was all Kizzy had ever looked for. Now she would get one more day, one last time.

"From what I know about Under Arches, I think they'd like to meet you," said Carolyn.

Kizzy called her mom and there was exactly the yelling and tears and apologies that she'd expected. It took a while. When she finally handed the phone back to Carolyn, they were driving through familiar city streets. The trip, which had been so epic on foot, was no distance at all by car.

Ned drove up to the parking spaces for the Constable Towers apartments, and Kizzy jumped out.

"Can I say good night to Do—to Pumpkin?" she asked.

"Of course you can. I'll double-check the latches afterward!" said Carolyn. She let down the back ramp and Kizzy climbed in.

Donut was standing in the darkness, pulling down mouthfuls of hay and chewing. Kizzy remembered the same sounds and smells from their first night together. She remembered waking in the night to watch his dark outline in her bedroom, and how happy she'd been.

But now he was somebody else's pony again. Kizzy found she couldn't say anything at all. She patted Donut's soft neck once, then turned and ran out of the trailer and toward Constable Towers. "Thanks," she managed to blurt to Ned and Carolyn over her shoulder before reaching the safety of the swing doors.

There had been a lot more yelling, but Kizzy knew her mom had almost forgiven her when she found a bag filled with sandwiches, chips, and an apple hanging off the front door handle when she went to let herself out early the next morning. There was a note attached:

"Supplies for the trip. Apple for pony from me. See you later to hear EVERYTHING." The last word was underlined three times.

Kizzy grabbed the bag with a smile and slipped quietly out of the apartment. It was still early: the time she would usually be taking Donut for his ride. Kizzy tried not to think about that. Traveling in the elevator without a pony was roomier and less nerve-wracking, but also less fun.

Crossing the lobby, Kizzy heard Mr. Newman's door open. She turned around and saw him bending down for his paper in his pajamas. He straightened up and looked at her. There was an uncomfortable pause.

"Did you get your bees back safely?" Kizzy asked him finally.

Mr. Newman nodded once. "I did. Need to start another hive for the new queen. New colony."

"That's good." Kizzy turned to go, but Mr. Newman coughed.

"Pony safely returned, too, is he?"

"Yes," said Kizzy.

"That's good," echoed Mr. Newman. "I might have

been a bit hasty yesterday. We don't need to say any more about it, do we? All's well that ends well."

"I guess. Thank you," said Kizzy. They smiled at each other. "Maybe I could help you with the new hive if you show me how?"

"Maybe you could," agreed Mr. Newman.

Outside, Ned and Carolyn were already waiting with the trailer. They waved and Kizzy ran to join them.

"Was he good overnight?" she asked.

"He was perfect," said Carolyn.

"Is he ready for the trip ahead? Will he be OK on his own? Because I could keep him company in there if it's going to be a long drive."

"I think he'll survive on his own. It's safer for you to stay in the car with us," said Ned.

Kizzy tried not to mind, although she wasn't sure what the point of coming was if she was barely going to see Donut. Maybe she was just prolonging the agony.

Ned started the engine and they drove off. Kizzy looked out the window. Everything had new memories now. It was painful. These were the streets that she'd cantered down yesterday; there was the supermarket; there was the street where Pawel lived—she definitely owed him a visit later. There was the park and her school and the shortcut to the old gas tank site. The familiar spots disappeared into the rearview mirror. Kizzy thought she heard Donut thump his hoof against the wall of the trailer, as if saying goodbye. They turned a couple of corners and—

"We're here," said Ned, slowing down and pulling up. They were on a dead-end side street. "Hope we're not too early."

"Here?" said Kizzy. "How can we be here? We've been driving less than ten minutes. We're still in the city— we're still in my neighborhood."

"See for yourself," said Ned, pointing. "Welcome to Under Arches Farm!"

At the end of the street, almost hidden away, was a tall, freshly painted rainbow-striped fence. A door had been cut into it and a sign above read: UNDER ARCHES FARM.

Kizzy stayed glued to her seat.

"Go on!" Carolyn nudged her. Kizzy climbed out and pushed through the small door.

Behind it, Kizzy found a secret world. Her first sight was of a central brick courtyard with animal

pens and paths leading off it. It was busy, like Plum Orchard, although not quite as clean. Despite the early hour, a handful of adults were carrying planks of wood, hammering and sawing, raking shavings, and painting signs. There were wheelbarrows of manure and buckets of feed lying everywhere. Chickens and ducks and a giant turkey were wandering about, getting under the feet of the people working. Kizzy noticed a pen with a pair of cute pink-and-black splotched pigs rooting around in mud, and another with goats in a range of sizes.

And then Kizzy saw what was behind the courtyard: inside the redbrick Victorian railway arches that supported an abandoned train line above, stables had been installed. A row of comfortable-looking stalls had been built into the arches; heads were already poking over the top of three of them.

"Hello, Mr. Snaffles, Twinkle, and Dumpty!" said Carolyn, coming up behind Kizzy and waving to the horses. "How are you settling into your new home? We've brought an old friend back to you. Pumpkin's been having adventures."

"He certainly has by the look of it!" A man in his twenties with a head of dreadlocks put down his saw and came toward them, smiling. "I was catching up on YouTube last night after you called me, Carolyn. You must be Kizzy, our famous local pony smuggler!"

Kizzy blushed and looked down, embarrassed, but he shook her hand in a friendly way. "I'm Stephen. I'm the farm manager here at Under Arches. We're still a couple of weeks away from officially opening our doors, but we're getting there!"

"I didn't know," said Kizzy. Her whole world had gone floaty and unreal.

"We're pretty excited about it, but the publicity campaign's late getting into gear," said Stephen. "It's been nonstop hard work since we got the grant. With all the animals starting to arrive and being settled in, everything is coming together. Just need some kids now!" He grinned at Kizzy.

"Kids?"

"Of course! This is a farm for the community—for everybody. We'll invite local schools and playgroups, show them where eggs and milk come from, and give riding lessons! You're going to help with those, aren't you, Carolyn? But we'll need a lot of volunteers to make it work." Stephen paused and studied Kizzy. "Interested in signing up? There might be some free rides in it. . . ."

"Interested?" said Kizzy. She could see Ned leading Pumpkin-Donut into the stable through a side gate—into his brand-new stall. "Am I interested? You could say I'm interested. Yes. YES. Oh, yes please, please, PLEASE!"

CHAPTER TWENTY

Kizzy had always dreamed she'd get a pony. But she had never, ever, ever dreamed that she would get four ponies.

Well, three ponies and a horse, because Mr. Snaffles was enormous. And they weren't strictly speaking hers, but who cared about that? Nobody was going to love them and take care of them better than she was.

She stepped through a bright door in a rainbow fence that had already become familiar, her mom and Jem following. The three of them stood for a moment, watching all the people gathering, the banner being unfurled and the tables being set up. Today was Under

Arches' official opening. Kizzy, who had been working hard to help get everything ready, hadn't stopped grinning for weeks. She thought she might never stop grinning.

"I'm just going to put these on the table, Mom. I hope they sell out—we're going to need to keep fundraising." Kizzy placed the heaped plate she was carrying down on one of the tables.

"I see Mr. Newman's donated some jars of his honey," said her mom.

"Yes! He's hoping he can start another hive here. Then everyone who comes can learn about bees, too."

"Kizzy! Kizzy! Kizzy! When can we ride?" Ali and Lopa ran into the yard and hugged her. Kizzy could see Mr. and Mrs. Kozlow and baby Marek behind them. For once, all three of them were smiling—Marek was finally growing out of his colicky stage.

"There's going to be a ribbon cutting and speeches first," said Kizzy. "Then you can sign up for lessons. And Pawel and I are going to lead some trips up and down the old railroad line. Come and choose who you want to ride."

"Can we meet all the ponies? And say hello to Donut—or is he called Pumpkin again now?"

"I can't get used to Pumpkin," admitted Kizzy. "Luckily he answers to Dokin and Pumpnut or anything really if you're giving him his hay. I'll take him one of these and we can see if he's a cannibal." Kizzy took a donut off her plate.

"What are they?" asked Lopa.

"Pumpkin donuts, of course! Hope he likes them. They've turned out a bit gooey."

"Donut won't care," said Ali.

"Hi, Kizz." Pawel popped up from behind one of the stall doors. "Turning up for the glory after I've done the hard work, are you? Typical. I've picked out Mr. Snaffles's hooves like you showed me, but I've left Twinkle for you. Twinkle scares me."

Pawel was dwarfed by Mr. Snaffles, a great bay horse who leaned out of the stall smacking his enormous soft lips. Ali and Lopa craned up on their tiptoes to pat him.

"Twinkle can be grumpy. You need to be careful with her," Kizzy explained to the girls. "You're fine with Mr. Snaffles though—he's a big softy."

"Is Twinkle the little black spotted one?" asked Ali, looking down the row.

"Piebald! Get your horse terminology right, Ali," corrected Pawel.

"You have learned well, my young pony padawan. Proud I am," said Kizzy in her best Yoda voice. "No,

Ali, the piebald one is Dumpty. Twinkle is the gray one with the rolling eye and her ears pinned back."

"I like Twinkle. I've decided: she's going to be my favorite," said Lopa. "Maybe she wants someone to cover her in glitter and stickers and brush her mane?"

"Maybe. Don't forget there are more ponies coming next month. But I know who my favorite is and always, always will be."

They had reached Pumpkin-Donut's stable. His head was out waiting for Kizzy, or possibly waiting for his pumpkin donuts. He practically inhaled it before accepting all of Kizzy's kisses. She couldn't resist bringing him out of his stable to show him all the fun.

"Under Arches Farm is like a fairy tale," said Lopa. "There's the Billy Goats Gruff, Chicken Little, and the Three Little Pigs — or the Two Little Pigs anyway."

They all looked around at the other animals. A lot of farm had been squeezed into either side of the arches. A path on one side led to a long, thin paddock. It was empty at the moment, waiting for some rare-breed sheep who would arrive later, but it would be used by the ponies, too. Beyond that was the riding arena: smaller than Kizzy's gas tank version, but covered in soft footings and better designed for lessons. The horses could also be ridden along a section of the old disused railway above them, which had been given official bridle path status. Under Arches Farm wasn't fancy or large, but everything had been thought of—a small patch of countryside right in the middle of the city.

"It's exactly like a fairy tale," agreed Kizzy.

Stephen, the farm manager, climbed on top of an old barrel in the middle of the yard. A red ribbon had been tied diagonally across the space. He banged a feed bucket.

"Can I have your attention, please?" he called. "It's been a long road for Under Arches to get here. There are many people to thank for all their hard work and help. But before I get to that long list, because you might want to settle yourselves into a seat with a snack to listen to it"—there was warm laughter—"I think we should be officially opened, don't you?"

Kizzy, Pawel, and everybody else cheered their agreement.

"It gives me great pleasure to welcome one of Hope Green's longest-standing residents to do the honors — someone who can remember when some of the animals we've brought to live here now were a common sight on the city's streets. I'm delighted to introduce the new official friend of Under Arches Farm, Miss Dora Turney!"

Stephen handed a pair of scissors to Miss Turney. She was looking very nice wearing shoes and a dress instead of slippers and a bathrobe. She'd had her hair done, too.

"Thank you. It's lovely to be here. It does make me think of my Robbie and the old days when there were plenty of . . ."

Kizzy waited for the familiar lines. Miss Turney stopped herself instead and smiled.

"Ah, I remember all the stories today. But as I'm going to be coming here often to share them, we'll leave them for now, huh? Let's get on with the party!" She cut the ribbon in half. "Under Arches Farm is open!"

There were more cheers and applause. People made
for the stands to buy coffee and snacks and plant seed-
lings. A steel band began to play. Ali and Lopa ran off
to dance.

"Shall we get the other ponies out and start leading rides?" Kizzy asked Pawel.

"I can't believe you've talked me into doing this. What have you done to me?" said Pawel.

"You're not fooling anyone. You love it here, too."

"Never mind your horses; I like the goats. They're funny. I might be a goatherd when I grow up," said Pawel. "Do you miss having Donut all to yourself, though? Are you going to mind taking other people for a ride rather than riding yourself?"

"I'll always miss him a little, but that's fine. This is the best place for him," said Kizzy. "And I rode Donut last night. Carolyn gave me my first real lesson. Guess what—we not only cantered, we jumped!"

"You jumped? Next stop the Olympics!"

"It was only a pole on the ground, but yes, definitely. Or maybe the Horse of the Year Show first for practice, and then the Olympics," agreed Kizzy. They bumped fists to settle it. "Anyway, Stephen says we should tack up Donut and Dumpty to start with."

Kizzy asked Jem to hold Donut while she went with Pawel to get everything they needed from Under Arches' tack and equipment shed. Riders coming here would be able to borrow everything, including helmets. Kizzy was picking up Donut's brand-new saddle when she heard a commotion outside. There was the sound of smashing plates. The steel band stopped playing abruptly. Kizzy heard someone shout, "Loose horse!" She dropped the saddle and raced out.

Donut was standing over what had been the snack table and was now a piece of wood on its side. With his tail swishing dreamily and a soft glint in his big brown eyes, he was head down in Kizzy's plate of pumpkin donuts, making them disappear like a magic act. Broken cups and plates, bits of brownie, and squashed sandwiches were scattered all across the yard. It was a scene of devastation. The people gathered were standing in shock while the farm chickens, ducks, and turkey flocked in, squawking wildly, to make the most of the feast on the ground.

"There was nothing I could do!" said Jem. "I only looked at my phone for a second, and he pulled the rope right out of my hands."

"Donut!" said Kizzy.

Donut's head came up at Kizzy's voice. His muzzle and whiskers were covered in sticky goo and crumbs.

The pony whickered softly, stepped daintily over the collapsed table, and walked over. He gently nudged against Kizzy's forehead with his donut-coated nose, leaving a mark like a lipstick kiss, then stood beside her. His breath was warm against her face. He smelled of pumpkin, honey, and oats.

Kizzy picked up his trailing rope. She looked at her shaggy-maned, toffee-colored, completely unrepentant miracle pony. He looked back at her. What was it Miss Turney had once said? "We all love our ponies, whatever they do." Something like that, anyway.

And it was perfectly true.